'Leave it to me,' he said. 'I will deal with it. Trust me to get you through this.'

'But why should you want to?' she asked, realising it was a question she should have asked a whole lot sooner than this. 'Why should it interest you at all?'

His answering smile was the cynical one. 'Come on, Francesca, the answer to that one must be perfectly clear,' he mocked as he moved one of his long thumbs to send it on a sweep of her now pulsing not quivering mouth. 'I want you for myself,' he told her grimly. 'Therefore I will do what it takes to get you.'

Then he was lowering his mouth again, to show how much he wanted her with yet another full-blooded, mind-blowing kiss.

Michelle Reid grew up on the southern edges of Manchester, the youngest in a family of five lively children. But now she lives in the beautiful county of Cheshire, with her busy executive husband and two grown-up daughters. She loves reading, the ballet, and playing tennis when she gets the chance. She hates cooking, cleaning, and despises ironing! Sleep she can do without, and produces some of her best written work during the early hours of the morning.

Recent titles by the same author:

THE SALVATORE MARRIAGE
A PASSIONATE MARRIAGE*
THE ARABIAN LOVE-CHILD*
ETHAN'S TEMPTRESS BRIDE*
THE SHEIKH'S CHOSEN WIFE*

Hot-Blooded Husbands

THE PASSION BARGAIN

BY
MICHELLE REID

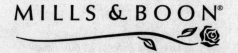

MILLS & BOON

*First published in Great Britain 2004
Harlequin Mills & Boon Limited,
Eton House, 18-24 Paradise Road, Richmond, Surrey TW9 1SR*

© Michelle Reid 2004

ISBN 0 263 83743 2

*Set in Times Roman 10½ on 11¼ pt.
01-0604-57232*

*Printed and bound in Spain
by Litografia Rosés, S.A., Barcelona*

CHAPTER ONE

FRANCESCA used gentle pressure on the brake pedal to bring the Vespa to a smooth stop at a set of red traffic lights then stretched out a long golden leg and placed a strappy-sandalled foot on the ground to maintain the motor scooter's balance while she waited for the lights to change.

It was a gorgeous morning, still early enough for the traffic on the Corso to be so light that she actually seemed to have the road almost entirely to herself.

A rare occurrence in this mad, bad, traffic-clogged city, she mused with a smile as she tossed back her head to send her tawny brown hair streaming down her back then closed her warm hazel eyes and lifted her face up to the sun to enjoy the feel of its silky warmth caressing her skin.

The air was exquisite today, clear and sharp and drenched in that unique golden light that gave Italy its famous sensual glow.

Her smile widened, her smooth rather generous mouth stretching to enhance the sheen of clear lip-gloss that along with a quick flick of mascara was the only make-up she wore.

Life, she decided, could not be more perfect. For here she was, living in one of the most beautiful cities in the world and only days away from becoming formally betrothed to the most wonderful man in the world. One very short month from now she and Angelo would be exchanging their marriage vows in a sweet little church overlooking Lake Alba before taking off for Venice to honeymoon in the most romantic city in the world.

And she was happy, happy, happy. She even sighed that happiness up at the sun while she waited for the lights to change, too engrossed in the warmth of her own sublime contentment to be aware of the sleek red sports car drawing up at her side. It was only when the driver decided to send the car's convertible top floating into its neat rear housing and the sultry sound of Puccini suddenly filled the air that she took note of his presence.

Then immediately wished that she hadn't when she took a glance sideways and saw *why* the driver had sent the car hood floating back. Her skin gave a sharp warning prickle, her soft hazel eyes quickly lost their smile—none of which had anything to do with the way she was being thoroughly scrutinised from the tips of her extended toes to the shiny flow of her freshly washed hair. Heck, it was almost obligatory for any warm-blooded Italian male to check out the female form when presented with the opportunity. No, her prickling response was due to the fact that she knew this particular Italian male. Or, to be more accurate, she had made his acquaintance once or twice when they had been thrown into the same company.

'Buon giorno, Signorina Bernard,' he greeted, the beautifully polite tones of this supremely cultured male completely belying the lazy sweep his dark eyes had just enjoyed.

'Signor,' she returned with a small acknowledging dip of her head.

If he noticed the chill she was giving off then he chose to ignore it, preferring to divert his attention away from her to guide one of his long-fingered hands out towards the car dashboard. Puccini died into a slumberous murmur. As he moved, sunlight shot across the raven's-wing quality of his satiny black hair. Signor Carlo Carlucci was a man that most people would describe as truly handsome, Francesca acknowledged with a complicated pinch of her stomach muscles that forced her to twitch restlessly. Skin the shade of ripened dark olives hugged the most superbly balanced bone structure she had ever seen on a man. Every one of his lean features quite simply fitted, even the nose that was so Roman you could not mistake his heritage. His jaw-line was square, his chin cleft, his cheekbones ever so slightly chiselled, and the firmly moulded shape of his slender mouth was—well—perfect, she admitted with yet another restless twitch.

Dark brown eyes were set beneath a pair of almost straight, satiny black eyebrows and were shaded by eyelashes that were almost a sin they were so long, and silky black. And as he shifted his long lean torso in the seat so he could give her his full attention Francesca would have had to be immune to the whole male species to resist noticing the leashed power in his muscles as they flexed beneath the bright white cloth of his shirt.

He oozed class and style and an unyielding self-possession. Everything about him was polished and smooth. He disturbed her when he shouldn't. He *antagonised* her when she knew she shouldn't let him.

Even the strictly polite smile he offered her set her nerve-ends singing as he remarked pleasantly, 'You were looking the essence of happiness as I drove up. I suppose credit for this must go to the fine weather we are enjoying today.'

If it was, now it's gone, Francesca thought resentfully. And wished she understood why she always suffered this itchy suspicion that he was taunting her whenever he spoke to her. He had been making her feel like this from the first time they'd been introduced at a party given by Angelo's parents. Even the way he had of looking at her always gave her the uncomfortable impression that he knew things about her that she did not and was amused by that.

He was doing it now, holding her gaze with his velvet dark eyes that pretended to be friendly but really were not. He mocked her—he *did*.

'Summer has arrived at last,' she agreed, willing to play the weather game that was what it took to keep this unwanted interlude neutralised long enough for the lights to change.

'Which is why you are out and about so early.' He nodded gravely, mocking her—again?

'I'm out and about early, as you put it, because this is my day off and I have things to do before I can hit the shops before the crowds arrive.'

'Ah.' He nodded. 'Now I understand the happy essence. Shopping has to be the preferred option to herding weary tourists through the Sistine Chapel or encouraging them to squat upon the Spanish Steps.'

He really had this taunting stuff down to a fine art, Francesca acknowledged as he put her right on the defensive. She had been guiding British tourists round the historical sites of Rome for months now and had learned early on that, though the city's economy might enjoy the healthy fruits of its tourist industry, the true residents of Rome did not always treat this point with the respect it deserved. They despaired of tourists, could be gruff and curt and sometimes downright rude. Especially in the high season, when they couldn't walk anywhere without bumping into camera-toting groups.

'You should be proud of your heritage,' she censured stiffly.

'Oh, I am—very proud. Why should you think that I am not? I simply object to sharing,' he said. 'It is not in my nature.'

'Which sounds very selfish.'

'Not selfish but possessive of what I believe belongs to me.'

'That still adds up to being selfish,' she insisted.

'You think so?' He took a second or two to contemplate that declaration. As he did so he shifted his body again, drawing her gaze to the white-shirted arm he lifted to rest across the black leather back of his seat. Long brown fingers with blunted fingernails uncoiled from a loose clench then rose upwards, tugging her trapped gaze with them as he brought them to rest against the smooth golden sheen of his freshly shaved cheek. He was gorgeous. Her mouth ran dry. Her tummy muscles pinched again and she became suddenly very aware of the Vespa's little engine vibrating between her spread thighs.

'No, I cannot agreed with you, *cara.*' He began speaking again, making her eyelashes flicker as her attention shifted to his moving lips. 'When I am involved in a deeply serious relationship with someone, would you still think it selfish of me to expect my lover to remain completely faithful only to me?'

Was he involved in a deeply serious relationship? For some mad reason her skin began to heat. Oh, stop it, she thought crossly. What was the matter with her? She had absolutely no excuse to get so hot and bothered over a man she didn't even like. She hardly knew him—didn't want to know him. The Carlo Carluccis of this world were way out of her league and she was happy to keep it that way.

'We were talking about Rome,' she pointed out curtly and flipped her eyes towards the set of traffic lights, willing the stupid things to hurry up and change.

'We were? I thought we had moved on to discuss my objection to sharing,' he murmured lazily. Teasing her— taunting her, she was sure—but why? 'Are you prepared to share your lovers, Francesca?' he dared to ask her. 'If I was *your* lover, for instance, would you expect me to be faithful only to you?'

This was stupid—stupid! I hate you, she told the stubborn red traffic light. 'Since there is no chance of that happening, *signor*, I don't see the use in discussing it,' she announced in her coldest, primmest English voice.

'Shame,' he sighed. 'And here I was, about to test my luck by suggesting that we continue this discussion in more congenial surroundings…'

Congenial…?

It was a clear come-on. Francesca was shocked enough to slew her widened eyes back to his face. It was a mistake. Her breath caught. Those warning prickles began racing up her spine because those dark, hooded eyes were travelling the length of her outstretched leg again. The sun-drenched air was suddenly charging up with sense-invading atoms that made the inner layers of skin covering her leg tingle as if he'd reached out with one of those hands and stroked right along its smooth golden length.

She almost gasped out loud at the electric sensation. The urge to whip her leg out of sight was almost too strong to stop. It took all of her control to keep the leg exactly where it was as she became stiflingly aware of the way her white cotton skirt was stretched taut across her slender long thighs.

Stop it! she wanted to shout at him. Stop trying to do this to me! But she found she couldn't manage a single stuttered word and those eyes were moving on; heavy-lidded, darkly lashed, they began slowly skimming her little blue sun top where her rounded breasts pushed at the finely woven cloth. Her nipples responded, tightening with piercing speed. The shock of it held her utterly transfixed as those dark eyes lifted higher until—shockingly—their gazes clashed.

He wanted her. The realisation hit her like a violent blow to the chest. Heat enveloped her from feet to hairline. Those eyes told her he knew what was happening to her and, worse, they were doing nothing to hide the fact that the same thing was happening to him. She could feel the sexual tension in his body, could see it burning in his now blacker than black eyes. Messages began leaping across the tarmac road and to her horror that place between her thighs feathered a ripple of pleasure across the sex-sensitive tissue.

It was so awful she shifted her hips with an uncontrollable jerk. In all of her twenty-four years she had never experienced anything as sexually acute as this. For a few more terrible seconds the world seemed to be closing in on her.

She couldn't breathe, couldn't think, couldn't move, couldn't—

'Have coffee with me,' he murmured suddenly. 'Meet with me at Café Milan…'

Have coffee with me, she repeated slowly to herself, her brain so sluggish that the invitation made no sense. Then it did make sense with all of its hot and spicy meaning. She grabbed at some oxygen. A car horn sounded. The real world came crashing back in. Dragging her eyes away from his, she looked blankly at the traffic lights, saw they'd turned to green and gunned the Vespa's little engine and took off down the Corso like a terrified pigeon in flight.

A top-of-the-range Lamborghini could outstrip a Vespa without any effort but, ignoring the protesting car horns behind him, Carlo remained exactly where he was.

His eyes were narrowed and fixed on the racing scooter and its beautiful rider, whose silky hair was blowing out behind her as she fled. He'd scared her out of her wits, Carlo acknowledged. Had he meant to do that? He was not entirely sure what his real motives had been, only that he had been presented with an opportunity and had used it—ruthlessly. Now pretend that I barely exist, *signorina*, he thought grimly.

The muted sound of Puccini rising to a crescendo began to infiltrate his consciousness. Reaching out, he hit the volume control to fill the air with the music then set the powerful car into motion again. There was a fine film of sweat bathing his torso beneath the fine cloth of his crisp white shirt and he grimaced. Francesca Bernard was the most excitingly sensual woman he had ever encountered and there was no way he was going to let all of that sensuality be laid to waste on a crass, mercenary fool like Angelo Batiste.

As the car built up speed along the Corso the Vespa had already turned off at a junction and by the time Carlo passed that junction neither bike nor rider were anywhere to be seen.

Francesca had pulled into a small piazza, cut the engine then climbed off the machine. She was feeling so shaken up inside that her legs felt like jelly, and she headed for the nearest café so she could sit down. A waiter appeared and she ordered fresh orange juice. She desperately needed a cup of strong coffee to calm her shattered senses but the very idea of drinking coffee was out of the question now that Carlo Carlucci had given the simple pleasure a whole new twist.

She shivered, still gripped by the shock of what had just happened. The whole incident had turned her into such a mess inside she could still feel those hot little *frissons* chasing across her skin. If he'd actually reached out and touched her she had a horrible feeling she would have gone up in a flaming orgasm. She had no idea where it had all come from. How it had gone from a simple tit-for-tat conversation at a red traffic light to—to what it did!

Her throat felt ravaged. She didn't think she'd managed to take a single breath all the way from those wretched lights until she sat down on this seat. Her hands were trembling, her legs, her arms—the tips of her stinging breasts!

It wasn't as if they even knew each other well enough to be anything more than polite nodding acquaintances! They'd met—what—twice before, maybe three times at most? And she didn't even like him. He had a way of antagonising her with that smoothly sardonic manner of his.

Her orange juice arrived. She nodded her thanks to the waiter then picked it up and gulped at it. The cool drink helped to soothe her throat but the rest of her didn't feel any relief.

Putting the glass down on the table, she hunched forward to sit there frowning into it. It was just beginning to dawn on her how easily she had let him get away with what he'd done. Usually she would know exactly how to deal with a teasing Italian who was only out to fill in a few empty seconds by having a bit of fun with her.

But Carlo Carlucci was no ordinary teasing Italian. He was the thirty-five-year-old head of the famous Carlucci Electronics. That placed him more than a decade ahead of her in years and eons ahead of her in every other way she could think of. Women adored him. He was rarely seen out without some acknowledged beauty hanging on his expensive arm. Put him in a room packed full of his tall, dark, handsome peers and he still managed to overshadow them all.

He was special. Even here in super-sophisticated Rome he was the man other men wanted to emulate. In the way these things should work, a lowly tour-guide like herself should never have come into contact with him at all. But Angelo was the son of one of Signor Carlucci's business associates, which meant they'd happened to find themselves in the same company while attending the same parties over the last few weeks. Not that this placed them in the same circles because it didn't, she reminded herself with a frown. Even Angelo only received a cool nod in acknowledgement from Carlo Carlucci's sleek, dark, sophisticated head. Angelo's father's company relied on Carlucci's for the main thrust of its business and Angelo was only a few years older than herself, which made him very junior and insignificant in the pecking order at these bright and sparklingly sophisticated social events.

But at least Angelo was warm and gentle and easy-going. He preferred fun to passion. It was years since a man like Carlo Carlucci had weaned himself off anything so juvenile as *fun*.

He was way out of her league, and anyway, she loved Angelo.

Yet when it really came down to the bottom line of it, she hadn't given a single thought to Angelo while she'd been thinking of Carlo Carlucci at that wretched traffic stop sign.

'Oh.' She choked on a fresh wave of *frissons*, which were

quickly doused by a heavy blanket of guilt. How could she—how *could* she have forgotten about Angelo at that wretched set of lights?

On impulse she reached into her tote bag to fish out her cellphone with the intention of calling up the man she loved. She needed to reassure herself that what Carlo Carlucci had just made her feel was nothing more than a blip on her hormonal calendar. She needed desperately to hear his warm, loving voice!

His cellphone was switched off. It was then that she remembered that he had business in Milan today. He was catching the early flight and had predicted he would be unreachable all day.

Then, *'Milan,'* she repeated and shuddered as the name conjured up a whole new meaning that placed it like *coffee* in the realms of sin.

Oh, stop it, she thought and tossed her cellphone onto the table then sat back in her seat and closed her eyes to work very hard at building Angelo's beloved golden image over the top of the darker one that should not have found a way into her head at all!

Angelo didn't have a dark corner in him. He was all sunlight. Golden skin, golden eyes and fine golden strands streaking in his tawny hair that she so loved to trail her fingers through. When he walked into a room he didn't cast a long shadow over everyone else, he lit it up with his warm golden temperament that had not yet become hidden beneath a hard, sophisticated shell. When he looked at her she felt warm and loved and beautiful, not—invaded by dark, untrammelled lusts.

Oh, all right, so she admitted it. Sometimes she'd wondered why their relationship wasn't more passionate. In fact, they had yet to actually make love.

'Time for that when you're ready,' she could hear his gentle voice saying.

And he was right because she wasn't ready. He'd understood from the beginning that she needed time to get used to the idea of full physical love. It wasn't that she was frigid, she quickly assured herself, just—wary of the unknown.

It came from being brought up by a deeply religious and straight-laced mother who'd instilled in her daughter standards by which she expected Francesca to live her life. Those standards included the sanctity of marriage coming before any pleasures of the flesh.

Outmoded principles? Yes, of course, principles like those were so out of fashion they could appear almost laughable to some. Indeed Sonya, her best friend and flatmate, did laugh at her—often. Sonya couldn't believe that a gorgeous masculine specimen like Angelo put up with a shrinking violet from a different century.

'You must be mad to play Russian roulette with a man like him,' she'd told her. 'Aren't you terrified that he might take his sexual requirements somewhere else?'

Well, yes, sometimes. She'd even confided those concerns to Angelo. He'd just smiled and kissed her, said Sonya was jealous and she wouldn't recognise a principle if she was staring at one.

Angelo didn't like Sonya. Sonya could not stand him. They provoked each other like two enemies across a neutral zone. Francesca was the neutral zone. The old-fashioned girl with the old-fashioned principles who loved them both but—more to the point—they loved her.

A smile crossed her mouth again. It wasn't quite as sunny as the smile she had been wearing before she ran into Carlo Carlucci but at least it was a smile.

Her telephone beeped, she twisted it around to check who was calling and the smile became a rueful grin. 'Were your ears burning?' she quizzed.

'Meaning what?' Sonya demanded, then sourly before Francesca could offer an answer, 'I suppose by that you're somewhere with darling Angelo and he's slandering my character again.'

'No,' Francesca denied. 'Angelo's in Milan today so put your claws away and tell me what you're ringing me for.'

'Do I only ring you when I want something?'

'The honest answer to that is—yes,' Francesca answered drily.

'Well, not this time,' her flatmate countered. 'I got up this morning to find you'd already left the flat. Why are you out so early? This is supposed to be your day off.'

'And you should be on your way to work by now.' Francesca took a quick glance at her watch. 'What time did you crawl into bed this morning?' It was definitely long after she had fallen fast asleep.

Her answer was a mind-your-own-business tut. 'Stick to the point,' Sonya snapped. 'Where are you going and how long will you be gone for?'

'I decided to come into town and do my shopping before it gets too hot and sticky to try on clothes.'

'Oh, I forgot. It's find-the-right-dress-to-knock-dear-Angelo's-eyes-out day.'

She really was obsessing on the man. 'Oh, do stop it, Sonya,' she sighed impatiently. 'Have you any idea how wearing this war between you and Angelo is? I hope you're going to call a truce before the party on Saturday night or I might just knock your heads together in front of Rome's best.'

'Maybe you would prefer it if I stayed away altogether— then you won't have to worry.'

She was offended now. Francesca uttered another sigh. 'Now, that's plain childish.'

'And you are beginning to sound like my mother. Don't do this, don't do that. At least try to behave yourself,' Sonya chanted deridingly. 'I hoped when I came to Rome that I would leave all of that stuff behind me in London.'

She was right, Francesca realised with a start—she sounded like her *own* mother. 'I'm sorry,' she murmured heavily.

'Forget it,' Sonya said and it was her turn to sigh. 'I'm a bitch in the mornings. You know I am. Go and buy your knockout dress and I'll crawl into work like a good girl.'

The call ended a few seconds later, leaving Francesca sitting there frowning and wondering what the heck had happened to her beautiful day.

The answer to that came in the form of a pair of dark eyes and a sensually husky voice saying, 'Have coffee with me at the Café Milan.'

A sudden breeze whipped up, swirling its way around the square, flipping tablecloths and shifting lightweight chairs. Francesca's hair was whipped backwards, her skin hit by a shivery chill. Then it was gone, leaving waiters hurrying to make good the disarray the breeze had left behind it and Francesca feeling as if she had just been touched by an ill wind.

She got up, took some money from her tote bag and placed it on the table to pay for her drink. As she walked back across the square to where she'd left the Vespa her skin was still covered in goose pimples yet she was trembling not shivering. She felt the difference so deeply it was almost an omen in itself.

CHAPTER TWO

IT WAS gone lunchtime by the time she arrived back at the apartment. As she stepped in through the door she then stood for a moment just looking around her in frowning puzzlement. The place had been quite tidy when she'd left here this morning but it didn't look like that now. The cushions on the sofa were crushed and tumbled. There were two half-drunk coffee-cups sitting on the low table and an empty bottle of wine with two glasses lying on their sides on the floor. She could see through the open door to Sonya's bedroom that it looked pretty much in the same tumbled state.

She was still frowning at the mess when her cellphone beeped and, placing her shopping bags on the floor, she fished out her phone to discover the caller was Bianca, the office manager of the tour group she and Sonya worked for.

She was looking for Sonya. 'She didn't turn up to work today,' Bianca announced. 'Have you any idea where she is? She isn't answering her mobile or the phone at your flat.'

Looking around at the evidence, Francesca could only assume that Sonya had been entertaining an unexpected visitor, though her loyalty to Sonya was not going to let her tell Bianca that.

'I'm sorry,' she said, 'but I left the flat before Sonya was up this morning so I've no idea where she is,' which wasn't a lie. 'Didn't she call in to warn you she wasn't going to make it?'

'No.' The manager's voice was tight. 'And she's left me a guide short. It really isn't on, Francesca. This is the third time in two weeks she's let me down like this.'

It was? Francesca's eyes widened at this surprise piece of information. She hadn't been aware that Sonya had been skipping off work. 'I know she's been suffering with a troublesome wisdom tooth lately,' which was true. Sonya complained about it a lot but was terror-struck at the mere mention of the word dentist. 'Maybe she couldn't stand the pain any more and went to get treatment.'

'And pigs might fly,' Bianca snapped. 'It's this man she has been seeing.'

Man? 'What man?' As far as she was aware, Sonya wasn't seeing anyone special at the moment.

'Don't pull the innocent, Francesca,' Bianca scolded. 'You know all about the married man she's lost her head over. If she's any sense she will drop him before this company drops her. I can't have my guides not turning up when they should. It makes an absolute mess of my...'

Francesca stopped listening, so stunned by the turn of this conversation that she had to sit down. She'd known Sonya since they'd been at university together and—OK, she acknowledged, so she was a bit of a rebel and tended to let her heart rule her head. But she confided most things to Francesca and she did not recall her saying a thing about a new man.

A *married* man?

Bianca had to be mistaken, she decided, only to look at the evidence laid out in front of her eyes that told her Sonya was up to *something* clandestine if she was resorting to skipping work so she could entertain her man here, where there was little chance of them being seen together.

'I'll come in and cover for her if you need me.' She cut across whatever it was Bianca was saying. She glanced at her watch. 'I still have time to get there if it will help you out.'

'Are you sure you don't mind? You were supposed to be shopping for your dress today. It doesn't seem fair that you should—'

'The dress is bought,' Francesca assured, glancing across the room to where she'd placed the elegant dress box that she'd ridden back here safely trapped between her legs. 'I'll be there as soon as I can make it.'

'You truly are an angel, Francesca,' Bianca said in relief. 'Unlike your wretched friend!'

The phone call ended. Francesca continued to sit there wondering what the heck had got into today. It had begun so well. She'd been happy—everything had been perfect!

Then Carlo Carlucci had happened, she recalled with a small shiver. Since her run-in with him nothing had gone right. She'd had phone calls that irritated, ill winds blowing chills across her skin and a tiring trudge through Rome's finest fashion boutiques, looking for a dress she still wasn't sure about even though she'd bought it. Now Sonya had gone missing and it was just beginning to dawn on her that, true to her flatmate's nature, she *had* rung her this morning to ask if she would cover for her at work. Only she'd then chickened out when they'd got into an argument over Angelo.

And now she had discovered that Sonya had been lying to her! Or keeping secrets was probably a fairer way of putting it.

But she didn't want to be fair. She didn't want to be *an angel* or have her best friend sniping at Angelo and then likening her to her mother because she happened to lose her patience.

More irritation struck, slicing right down her backbone and bringing her to her feet. She bent to pick up the used coffee-cups then stopped herself. Tidying up after Sonya was something her mother would do. So was tutting and sighing all over the place, as she'd been about to do.

'Oh, damn it!' she shouted at the tiny apartment. And she *never* swore!

Because her mother would have been appalled.

'Damn it,' she said again out of sheer black cussedness and went to put her purchases away.

Then she went still, listening to herself and not liking

what she heard. Her mother was gone now and she did not want to think ill of her. She didn't want to be sniping at her inside her head! There had been too much ill feeling in Maria Bernard's life while she had been alive, she thought bleakly as she went to unpack and hang up her dress.

Her mother had once been the beautiful Maria Gianni—only child of Rinaldo Gianni, a man who ran his household with a rod of iron. He'd woven plans around his only daughter that had mapped out her entire future from the day she had been born. Then Maria had thwarted those plans by falling in love with a thankless English rake called Vincent Bernard, who had his eye firmly fixed on Maria's inheritance. It had taken a month for him to make her pregnant and another month to get her father's permission to marry her—before Rinaldo Gianni threw them out. Vincent had taken her mother to England. He'd been so sure that his father-in-law would relent and forgive once Maria produced the grandson the old man wanted so much that he was prepared to wait the whole nine months for the event to take place. A girl had not fitted either man's criteria. Vincent Bernard had cut his losses and left Maria holding a baby girl that nobody wanted by then. A year after that Vincent had divorced her to marry his next rich fool of a wife. Divorce had been the ultimate humiliation and sin in her mother's eyes. She'd never acknowledged that legal slip of paper ending her Roman Catholic marriage. She'd never forgiven her father for refusing to forgive her for going against his wishes. All three had never spoken again.

Rinaldo Gianni had died when Francesca was ten years old, having never acknowledged that he had a granddaughter. She'd never met him, just as she had never met her own father, who—and here was the irony—died around the same time. It wasn't until a year after her mother's death that she'd given in to a long-suppressed yearning to come to Rome and meet with her only surviving blood relative. And even as she'd taken that first step onto Italian soil she had still been struggling with her conscience because she'd known her mother would not approve. But it was lonely being on her own yet knowing she had a great-uncle living here who might—just might—be prepared to welcome Maria's child.

She'd wanted nothing else from Bruno Gianni. Not his money or even his love. She hadn't got them either, she mused with a wry little smile as she dried herself after a quick shower. Her great-uncle Bruno, she'd discovered, was a very old man living the life of a near recluse in his draughty old *palazzo* tucked away in the Albany Hills south of Rome. He did not receive visitors. He did not have a great-niece, she was informed by return letter when she'd made her first tentative approach. It had taken determined persistence on her part before the old man eventually gave in and reluctantly granted her an audience.

It was a strange meeting, she recalled, pausing for a moment to look back to that one and only time she'd met Bruno Gianni. He was nice. She'd liked him on sight even though he had told her straight off that if she was after his money then there was none to be had. The crumbling *palazzo* belonged to the bank, he'd said, and what bit of money he had left would go to the tax collector when he was dead.

But she'd been able to see her mother's eyes in his eyes— her own hazel eyes looking curiously at her even as he'd labelled her a fortune-hunter. She recalled how badly she'd wanted to touch him but didn't dare, how his skin wasn't at all wrinkly despite his great age and he might live in a near ruin but his grooming had been immaculate. Quite dapper.

She smiled as she began dressing again, slipping into her uniform red dress with its flashes of bright yellow and green.

She'd told him about her life and her mother's life in London, the schools she'd attended and her university degree. She'd told him that she was working as a tour guide in Rome and that she was sharing an apartment with a friend she'd met in university. He'd listened without attempting to put a stop on her eager flow. When she'd finally slithered to a stop, he'd nodded as if in approval then rung the bell. When the housekeeper arrived to see her out all he'd said was, 'Enjoy the rest of your life, *signorina*,' and she'd nodded, knowing by those words that he had no wish to see her again.

That didn't mean she'd stopped corresponding though. She'd continued to send him little notes every week, letting him know what she was doing. When she'd met and fallen in love with Angelo, besides Sonya, Great-Uncle Bruno was the first person to know. He'd never replied to a single letter and she hadn't a clue if he even bothered to read her silly, light, chatty notes. When she confided in Angelo about him he was shocked and disbelieving at first, then he'd laughed and called their first meeting fate because Bruno Gianni lived only a couple of miles away from his parents' country house.

'If your mama had been allowed to live there with you, we would have grown up together—been childhood sweethearts maybe.'

She liked that idea. It gave their love a sense of inevitability and belonging that her unforgiving grandfather could not beat.

On the few occasions she had been invited to spend the weekend at the Villa Batiste in the Frascati area of Castelli Romani she always made a point of walking the few miles to her great-uncle's *palazzo* to leave a note to let him know where she was staying—just in case he might relent and asked her to visit him while she was there. It had never happened. He hadn't even bothered to reply to the formal invitation to her betrothal party this weekend, she reminded herself.

Did that hurt? A little, she confessed. But—as Angelo said—persistence could often win in the end. 'Maybe he will relent and come to our wedding.'

And maybe he would, she thought hopefully as she shut up the apartment and stepped back out into the sunlit street.

However disappointed she was with her great-uncle, she had never regretted coming to Rome. Her Italian was fluent, her knowledge of the city's history something she'd drenched herself in from the time she had been able to read. She loved her job, loved her life and she loved—loved Angelo.

The ride down the Corso was a mad, bad bustle this time around. Francesca skimmed deftly between tight lines of traffic. The afternoon was a long one. The city was beginning to throb with people now the tourist season was in full flow—not that it eased by a huge amount at any time of the year. By the time she arrived back at the apartment she was so tired all she wanted to do was dive beneath the shower then put up her aching feet.

The first thing she noticed was the tidied apartment, the next was Sonya, curled up on the sofa wrapped in her bathrobe, looking very defiant.

'Before you start, it was the toothache,' she jumped in before Francesca could say anything. 'It flared up after I spoke to you this morning and I just had to find a dentist to do something about it.'

'Makes house-calls, does he?' Francesca didn't believe her. It took only a flick of her eyes to the empty coffee-table for Sonya to know what she meant.

'Of course not,' she snapped then winced, pushing a hand up to cover the side of her face. 'God, it's hurting more now that the anaesthetic's worn off than it did before I let him touch it!' she groaned.

'*Who* touched it?'

'The dentist, you sarcastic witch,' Sonya sliced. Then she sighed when she realised she wasn't about to get any sympathy, her gentian-blue eyes moving over Francesca's clothes. 'Sorry I spoilt your day off,' she mumbled contritely.

'You meant to do that a whole lot earlier this morning,' she drawled.

'Mm.' Sonya didn't even bother to deny it; her fingertips were now carefully testing the slight puffiness Francesca could see at her jaw.

'You look grotty,' she observed, yielding slightly. 'How bad is it?'

'Really bad.' Tears even swam into her eyes. 'He drilled it then dressed it with—something.' She dismissed that *something* with a flick of her hand. 'I'm to go back next week—ouch.' She winced again. 'I also got the full lecture on the cause and effect of neglect.'

Francesca couldn't help but smile at the last dry comment. Sonya didn't like lectures especially when she had no defence. 'Did you punch him?' she asked.

'Not likely! He had me pinned down with all these contraptions sticking out of my mouth and was holding a drill in his hand at the time.'

'Poor you,' she commiserated.

'Mm.' Sonya was in complete sympathy with that comment. 'Did you get your dress?' she then thought to enquire.

'Mm,' Francesca mimicked. 'Did you get your intriguing new man to hold your hand while you sat in the dentist's chair?'

Sonya looked up then quickly away again, a definite flush mounting her delicately pale cheeks. 'Don't ask because I'm not going to tell you,' she muttered.

'So he *is* married,' Francesca concluded.

'Who told you that?' Sonya was shocked.

'Bianca,' she supplied. 'Who seems to know a whole lot more than I do about your love-life.'

That still hurt, and she turned away to walk towards her bedroom.

'I'm sorry, Francesca, but I *can't* talk about him!' she threw after her. 'It's—complicated,' she added awkwardly. 'And Bianca only knows the bit she gleaned out of me when she caught me rowing with him on the phone in the office the other day. '

'So he is married?' She turned to look at her.

Sonya looked down and stubbornly closed her mouth.

The urge to tell her what a fool she was being leapt to the edge of her tongue—then was stopped when she remembered the 'you sound like my mother' stab from this morning. So she changed her mind about saying anything at all and turned back to her bedroom.

'I'm going to change,' she said. 'I'm meeting Angelo in a hour—'

'No, you're not.'

Once again she stopped and swung round. 'What's that supposed to mean?'

'He rang here—a few minutes ago—to say he's still in Milan and won't be coming back until tomorrow.' For some reason relaying all of that also poured hot colour into her cheeks.

Francesca's eyes narrowed in suspicion. 'Have you two been fighting again?'

'No,' Sonya denied.

'Then why the guilty face?'

'OK, so we fought a little bit,' Sonya snapped. 'Stop getting at me, Francesca! I can't help it if—'

'So, why didn't he call me on my mobile to tell me this?' Francesca cut in. She was not going to let Sonya start one of her character-assassination jobs on Angelo again. One a day of those was enough.

'He said you weren't answering.'

Francesca glanced at her bag then went to recover it. The moment she fished inside the uniform brown leather satchel she knew why he couldn't reach her. In her rush that lunchtime she must have left the phone in her tote bag.

'Idiot,' she muttered and went into the bedroom to get it so she could return his call—only to find Sonya had followed her and was standing in the doorway, wearing the oddest expression on her face. Francesca couldn't quite read it—anxiety, pleading? Or was it pain from the tooth?

'Are you feeling all right, *cara*?' she probed gently. 'You look terribly flushed.' She put a cool palm against Sonya's cheek and was surprised just how hot she felt. 'At the risk of being accused of mothering you, would you like me to tuck you into bed and bring you a nice hot chocolate drink?'

The tears arrived then, turning gentian-blue into midnight pools in a face that was so classically beautiful it was no wonder she'd been screen tested by a film director once. 'Don't be nice to me, Francesca,' she murmured.

'I love you,' she smiled, moving her fingers into the straight, glossy pelt of her friend's long, flaxen hair. 'Why shouldn't I be nice?'

'Because I don't deserve it.' Sonya stepped away from her so she could use the sleeve of her bathrobe to wipe her eyes with. 'I use your friendship dreadfully.'

'Only because I let you.'

'Yes…' Sonya agreed and looked momentarily devastated. The phone went then, breaking the moment. Sonya went into the sitting room to answer it and a few seconds later was calling Francesca to come to the phone.

'*Ciao, mi amore.*' It was Angelo, his voice sounding weary and flat. 'You don't answer your cellphone because you don't want to speak to me and I cannot blame you.'

'I didn't have my phone with me so I couldn't answer it, you sweet idiot,' she chided, her eyes flickering sideways to watch Sonya disappearing into her bedroom. The moment the door shut behind her Francesca lowered her voice into soft, loving tones. 'I'm sorry you're stuck in Milan.'

'So am I,' he agreed. 'I am about to get ready to take dinner with some business colleagues when I should be on my way to share a romantic dinner with you. Ah, *misero*,' he declared feelingly.

'Poor *caro*,' she commiserated.

Angelo heaved out a sigh. 'But enough of this.' He firmly

pulled his mood out of the doldrums. 'Tell me about your day.'

'Well, my plans fell to pieces much as yours did…' She went to explain, leaving out the incident at the traffic lights and editing some of the more contentious events involving Sonya so she didn't invite him to vent his frustrations on the one person guaranteed to earn his wrath. 'But I did manage to find a dress for Saturday,' she finished on a high note.

To her surprise he made no cruel remarks about Sonya's toothache. In fact he skimmed right over the fact that she'd even been mentioned at all and asked about her dress instead. She refused to tell him and there followed a few minutes of soft teasing that was much more like the man she loved. Then he had to go and the call ended, leaving Francesca feeling loved and filled with that golden warmth that was her Angelo.

Sonya didn't come out of her bedroom again that evening. Francesca went in to check on her a couple of times but all she could see was the crown of her head peeping out from beneath a mound of duvet and eventually left her to sleep off the ordeal with the dentist.

By the next morning she was herself again and ready to face Bianca's wrath head-on. They rode down the Corso side by side on similar Vespas and dressed in the same red uniforms. Their day was busy as always.

Angelo called at lunchtime to break the news that he was going to be stuck in Milan for another night. The next day was Saturday and they were supposed to be driving into the Alban Hills together but that plan had to be shelved. 'I have arranged with my parents for you to travel with them,' he told her.

It wasn't a prospect that filled her with delight. She had discovered quite early on in her relationship with Angelo that his parents were not the kind of people who were ever going to welcome her with open arms. She harboured a suspicion that she was not what they'd been hoping for as a wife for their precious only son and if it wasn't for her very loose connection to the Gianni name they would have been actively against Angelo marrying her. As it was, Mrs Batiste had grilled her once about her mother, then surprised her by confessing that she and Maria Gianni had attended the same convent school. 'You look very like her—apart from the hair,' she'd said, Maria's hair having been as glossy Latin black as hair could be. 'I'm sorry she had such a difficult life, Francesca. I hope your marrying my son will give you a happier one—for Maria's sake—and that Bruno Gianni relents his foolish stubbornness one day for your sake. But until then I think we will not mention him again.'

And that had basically been it. The Gianni connection was smoothly sidelined, which suited Francesca because she didn't like talking about it and was happy to keep it that way.

The journey to Frascati wasn't too bad. Angelo's parents' manner towards her might be cool but it wasn't frigid. She loved Angelo, they loved Angelo, so that was their line of communication. They were almost at their destination when Angelo's mother voiced her annoyance that her son should have been held up in Milan this week of all weeks.

'It is his own fault,' her husband returned without any sympathy. 'Angelo knows it is not good business practice to keep busy people kicking their heels while they await his late arrival.'

'It wasn't as if he intended to be late. He overslept and missed the flight,' Angelo's *mama* defended loyally.

He did? thought Francesca. It was the first she'd heard of it.

'No one else missed the flight,' the father made the succinct distinction. 'Whatever *they* had been doing the night before, they still managed to get to the airport on time.'

In the back of the car Francesca shifted slightly, catching the attention of Mr Batiste via his rear-view mirror. 'My apologies, Francesca,' he said, 'I was not being critical of the late hours you young people keep, only Angelo's failure to rise from his bed when he should,' bringing a flush of heat into her face when she realised what he was assuming.

But it wasn't true. She hadn't seen Angelo the night before he went to Milan. Because of the early time of his flight he'd told her he was going to get an early night.

'We cannot afford to offend a man like Carlo Carlucci. His business is too important to us,' Mr Batiste went on, his attention back on the road ahead so he didn't see the way Francesca's face went from hot to pale at the mention of Carlo Carlucci's name. 'Being stuck in Milan while Carlo puts him through business hoops is a better punishment than to have Carlo take his business somewhere else.'

Mrs Batiste demanded her husband's attention then, with a comment that was spoken too low for Francesca to hear. It didn't matter because she had stopped listening anyway. She was thinking about Carlo Carlucci and that awful morning she had met him at a set of traffic lights. He must have been on his way to meet with Angelo at the airport yet he hadn't bothered to mention it—nor had it stopped him from making a play for her.

She shifted restlessly again, feeling the same hostile prickles attacking her skin as she replayed the ease with which he'd conducted that little scene.

What made the man tick that he felt he could do that to her, knowing what he knew? Arrogance? A supreme belief in his right to toy with another man's woman simply because it had amused him to do so? If she'd said yes to the coffee thing, would he have just laughed in her face and driven off, having got all the kicks he'd been looking for from the interlude by successfully seducing another man's woman? Or would he have been willing to miss *his* flight in favour of coffee with her at Café Milan?

Oh, don't go there, she told herself, frowning out of the car window as something low in her abdomen began to stir.

What about Angelo? She considered, firmly fixing her attention on what should be important here. Why hadn't he told her that he was stuck in Milan because he'd overslept and annoyed an important business client? Did he think that confessing he'd messed up would lose him his hero status with her?

A smile touched her mouth, amusement softening the frown from her face. He ought to know that nothing could do that. He was and always would be the wildly handsome superhero to her.

They arrived at their destination, driving between a colonnade of tall cypress trees towards the stunning white and gold frontage of Villa Batiste. It wasn't a big house by Castelli Romani standards but, standing as it did on its own raised plateau, neither the house nor its amazing gardens skimped on a single detail when it came to Renaissance extravagance.

As they climbed out of the car at the bottom of wide white marbled steps, Francesca could almost feel the Batistes filling with pride of ownership and wondered wryly—not for the first time—how that pride really dealt with Angelo wanting to marry a little nobody like her. He would inherit all of this one day, which would make her its chatelaine and her children its future heirs.

The house was already under the occupation of an army of professional caterers. A quick cup of coffee after their journey was all they had time for before they were busily helping out. Mr Batiste went off to check his wine cellar. Mrs Batiste made for the kitchen. Francesca became a willing dogsbody, helping out wherever she could. By two o'clock there was nothing more for her to do that she could see. Angelo was still stuck in Milan and his parents were resting before the next wave of activity began.

On a sudden impulse, she decided to write a note to her great-uncle then go and deliver it. You never know, she told herself as she set off, she might *just* catch him at a weak moment.

Her walk took her along narrow, winding country lanes with blossom trees shedding petals on the ground and the golden sunlight dappling through their gently waving branches. It was a beautiful place and she took her time, taking in the hills and the rolling wine-growing countryside that gave such a classic postcard image of Italy.

Half an hour later and she was standing by a pair of rustic old gates, gazing on a house and a garden that would make Angelo's mother shudder in dismay. There was nothing formal or neat about her great-uncle's garden, she mused with a smile. The whole thing seemed to merge in a rambling mix of untended creepers with the old *palazzo* struggling to hang on to some pride as its ochre-painted face peeled and its roof sagged.

She lingered for a few minutes, just looking at it all like a child forbidden to enter. She didn't think of opening the gate and stepping inside. She never intruded past this point when she came here because she knew it was only right that she respect her uncle's wishes. After a little while she heaved out a sigh then took her sealed note out of her jacket pocket and fed it into the rusted metal letter slot set into one of the stone pillars that supported the gates. As she listened to it drop she had the sorry image of the note landing on top of all the others she'd posted and a sad little smile touched the corners of her mouth as she turned slowly away.

Head down, shoulders hunched inside her fitted little denim jacket that matched the jeans she was wearing, she was about to begin the walk back to Villa Batiste when a flash of bright red caught her eye. Her chin came up then all movement was stalled on a stifled gasp of surprise and undisguised dismay when she saw an all too familiar red sports car parked up on the other side of the lane with its driver leaning casually against shiny red bodywork.

Oh, no, not him, was her first gut response as they stared at each other across the few metres of tarmac.

He was dressed in dark blue denims and cloud-blue cashmere that skimmed his tapered body like a second skin. The way he had arms folded across his chest ruched up the lip of the long-sleeved, round-necked sweater, exposing the bronze button that held his jeans in place and almost—almost—offered her a glimpse of the lean flesh beneath.

On a sharp flick of shock as to where her thoughts were taking her she dragged her eyes upwards to look at his face. He was smiling—or allowing his attractive mouth to adopt a sardonic lift. His chin was slightly lowered, his eyelashes glossing those chiselled bones in his cheeks. And he was checking her out in much the same way that she was guilty of checking him out, viewing the length of her legs encased in faded denim, then the fitted denim jacket and finally her face.

'Ciao,' he greeted softly—intimately—causing her next response to him, which was a shower of prickly resentment that raced across her skin.

'What are you doing here?' she demanded, not even trying to sound polite.

'We do seem to meet in the oddest of places,' he mused drily. 'Do you think, cara,' he added thoughtfully, 'that we might be the victims of fate?'

CHAPTER THREE

FATE, Francesca repeated to herself. She knew about the power of fate. Fate was what Angelo maintained had brought them together. She refused to accept that this…force she was being hit with here had any familiarity with Angelo's fate.

It was then that she remembered tonight's party and that this man had been invited. She'd even written the invitation herself. *Carlo Carlucci and Guest,* she'd scribed in Italian.

Which brought up another thought that sent her eyes slewing sideways to glance inside the open-top car expecting to see some raving dark beauty sitting in the passenger seat. To think of Carlo Carlucci without his usual female appendage was impossible, so she was puzzled to discover the seat was empty.

When she looked back at him he'd lifted those lashes higher and was watching her. 'I do travel light on occasion,' he said lazily, reading her like a gauche open book.

'Does the fact that you're here and not in Milan mean that you've tired of making Angelo's life a misery and let him come back too?' she threw back.

He smiled at this attempt on her part at acid sarcasm but his reply when it came was deadly serious. 'Angelo deserved everything he got from me, Francesca, and don't let him tell you otherwise.'

'I suppose you've never overslept and missed a meeting.'

'Not even after a heavy night with a beautiful woman in my bed,' he replied. 'Although…' his eyes moved over her '…I can appreciate that the cause in this case was worth the consequences…'

He was inferring that she was what had caused Angelo

34

to oversleep that morning, Francesca realised, and opened her mouth to deny the charge only to close it again when she realised that Angelo must have used her as his excuse for missing his flight. A frown creased her brow and she lowered her eyes to the ground while she tried to decide how she felt about that. She didn't think she liked it. It smacked too hard at the male ego conjuring up a night of erotic sex with his lover as a way of getting himself out of an awkward situation. Her mind even threw up a picture of Angelo standing in some faceless office in Milan, casually boasting to this man of all men about something that should remain private to themselves—if it had happened at all, which it hadn't.

'I've got to go.' She spun away, not wanting to continue this line of discussion. Not wanting to be here at all. She was cross now with Angelo—cross with Carlo Carlucci for placing a cloud across her golden image of the man she loved.

There was a hiss of impatience, a scraping of shoe leather on the road surface. 'Wait a minute,' he said, and began striding towards her across the lane.

Her shoulders tensed, her clenched hands jerking out of her pockets as those now familiar prickles began really asserting themselves the closer he came. A hand curved around her arm, long fingers gently crushing sun-warmed denim against the skin beneath that began to burn like a flame. She jumped in response to it, her breathing snagged. He turned her to face him and she found herself fascinated by the discovery that her eyes came level with his smooth brown throat.

'I embarrassed you. I apologise,' he murmured huskily, and she watched his throat muscles move with the words. 'It was unforgivably crass and insensitive of me to say what I just said.'

Yes, Francesca agreed. It had been crass and insensitive—but which man had been the most crass and insensitive?

'Forget it,' she said, but both of them knew she was only mouthing words she did not mean.

'If it helps, he did not mention you by name,' he offered.

'Meaning what?' she flashed. 'That he left it open to interpretation as to whether he was sleeping around or not? Great. Thanks.' She gave an angry tug at her arm.

He refused to let go. She could feel his anger, the pulse of his frustration because his bit of light teasing had gone so wrong.

'I apologise—again,' he bit out finally.

Francesca glared daggers at his chest. 'I suppose you think it's all just jolly good fun to swap sexual experiences across some office desk,' she said shakily. 'Men being men,' with lots of *phews* and *wows* and *you'd have overslept too if you'd been there.* She'd heard the men at work talking like that, having no idea how cheap they made their lovers sound. 'Egotistic cockerels crowing about their prowess,' she muttered, not realising she'd said the words out loud until he laughed as if he couldn't help himself.

'Don't laugh at me!' she snapped out hotly.

'Then don't say such comical things,' he threw back. 'You sound like some outraged virgin.'

But she was an outraged virgin—that was the whole point! 'Did you tell him all about the way you propositioned me on the Corso just to even up the score a bit?'

'No,' he denied. 'But the interesting point here is—did *you* tell him?'

'Why, are you worried that he might damage your famed sexual ego by telling him how you made a play for his woman and got turned down flat?'

It was reckless. She shouldn't have said it. His eyes turned as black as bottomless caverns and his other hand came up to capture her other arm. Hard fingers crushed the denim fabric as he drew her closer.

'Did you turn me down?' he prompted. 'Or did you run

like a frightened rabbit because you were already so turned
on you didn't know how to cope with it?'

'That's not true!' she gasped in shocked horror.

'Shall we test that?'

She saw in the dark glitter of his eyes what he meant to
do next and drew in a sharp breath. Suddenly something
dangerous was dancing in the air, spinning silver spider
webs of tension into the golden sunlight.

Then a twig snapped somewhere, bringing the whole ep-
isode clattering down as both heads turned to stare across
the top of her great-uncle's wooden gates. Trapped in a
trembling force field that held her breathless, Francesca
searched the wilderness in some wild, weak, pathetic hope
that her great-uncle was about to appear to rescue her from
this.

It didn't happen. No dapper old gentleman wearing a
wine-red velvet smoking jacket appeared on the twig-strewn
driveway. The dappling light from the afternoon sun quivered amongst the heavily leafed branches of the tangled
trees and vines and played with peeling ochre paint, but
otherwise the wilderness garden remained at peace.

She sighed as she thought that, the action parting her lips
to release the sad sound. He moved, she looked back at him
without thinking and met head-on with a pair of dark, brooding eyes that told her things she didn't want to know—or
feel the way she was feeling them.

It was better to look away. 'Please let me go,' she whispered shakily.

His fingers flexed against the denim and for a horrible
moment she thought he was going to ignore her plea and
just continue from where he'd been interrupted. Her throat
ran dry. She tried to swallow. The promise of tears bloomed
across her eyes.

Then his grip eased and slowly lifted. She stepped back—
went to turn her back, desperate now to get away.

'You are acquainted with Bruno Gianni?' he asked.

'What…?' She blinked, lifting slightly unfocused eyes back to his face. 'Oh, n-no,' she denied, and quickly lowered her eyes again—not because of the lie she'd just uttered but because she didn't want him to see the threatening tears.

She shoved her hands back in her pockets, swung away and made another attempt to leave.

'Strange…' he murmured. 'I could have sworn I saw you posting a note in the letter box as I drove up.'

And she froze all over again. 'Y-you mistook what you saw,' she said stiffly. 'I was admiring the garden, that's all.'

'The garden,' he repeated and uttered a soft laugh. '*Cara*, that isn't a garden, it is a neglected mess!'

'And what would you know about a real garden?' she swung round to slice at him, not sure if she was responding to his derision or the near kiss she had just escaped. 'I bet your idea of a beautiful garden has to be something filled with straight lines and must be manicured to within an inch of its life!'

'Bruno Gianni obviously doesn't feel like that,' he pointed out.

He was laughing—*still* laughing at her! He'd even leant a shoulder against one of the gateposts—right next to *her* letter box! And he'd folded those wretched arms again, tugging that jumper up over the bronze stud at his waist. She hated him, really hated every hard, mocking inch of his sardonic, handsome—*sexy* stance!

'Well, neither do I,' she declared, uttering this next half-lie as she tried very hard to put her temper back under wraps. 'And I like this garden,' she added within a tightly suppressed breath. 'I like the way it's been left to do its own thing. It has soul and atmosphere and—and—'

'An irresistible hint of romance about it,' he inserted when she stammered then stalled. 'We could even say it possesses a kind of lost-in-time mystique about it that some may love to weave secret fantasies around. We could even imagine Sleeping Beauty lying in one of the cobweb-strewn rooms inside waiting for her prince to come and waken her with the all-important kiss.'

'Oh, very droll,' she derided. 'Next you will be telling me you believe in fairies.'

'Why not?' he quizzed. 'We should all believe there is magic out there or we would stop bothering to look for it and that would be sad, don't you think? Oh, come on, Francesca,' he sighed out impatiently when she stiffened up in offence. 'I was teasing you. Stop prickling.'

'I'm not prickling,' she snapped, prickling even as she denied it.

He uttered a short laugh. 'You remind me of a very beautiful but temperamental tabby cat,' he told her. 'Every time I look at you I can almost see the hairs on the back of your neck standing up.'

'You don't know me well enough to know anything of the sort,' she hit back, saw the amusement lurking behind those glossy eyelashes, went to stiffen up some more—then sighed heavily instead. 'You enjoy winding me up.'

'*Sì,*' he acknowledged.

So she was a game, Francesca concluded. An *easy* game.

Carlo studied her beautiful face as she stood in her own pool of sunlight and wondered grimly if she had any idea how hurt she looked by his last comment. Anger gripped him, along with a hot and bloody frustrated urge to grab for her again and impress on her *why* his barbs could hurt so much.

Easy, he thought inwardly in grinding contempt and flicked a hard glance at the crumbling Palazzo Gianni hiding inside its romantic wilderness. Sleeping Beauty she was not; Cinderella more like, so damn starved of ordinary love and affection that she left herself wide open for any no-good adventurer to take advantage of.

Damn it, he cursed to himself and straightened away from the gatepost. 'I suppose,' he started, 'if I offer you a lift, you will throw the offer back in my face.'

He was right and she would. 'Take no offence but I will enjoy the walk.'

The sound of his dry laughter brought her reluctant gaze back to his face again. 'That was so beautifully English and polite, *cara*.' The mocking man was back, she saw.

'I am English.'

'Mm,' he murmured as if even that amused him now. Then he surprised her by abruptly striding back to his car. 'Like a cool breeze on a hot summer's day,' he threw over his shoulder as he opened the door then swung his long body into the seat. 'Very—contradictory.'

'Thank you—I think.' She frowned.

Carlo just grimaced and gunned the car engine. 'I will see you later,' he said by way of a farewell.

Francesca sent him a perfectly blank look.

'Your engagement to the mistreated Angelo?' he prompted and was truly rewarded when the blank look changed to one of dismay because that look told him she had not given a thought to her wonderful Angelo beyond those first few seconds of this encounter.

Having to be satisfied with achieving that much, he put the car into gear and sped off down the lane, leaving her to stew alone on his final heart-ruthless barb.

Francesca watched him go with the sunlight clinging to his satin black hair again and his last sardonic punch making her eyes blink. How could she have become so drawn in by him that she'd completely forgotten the most important event in her life was about to take place tonight?

Another twig snapped somewhere behind her and she turned to glare at her great-uncle's wilderness as if all of this confusion she was feeling was his fault. And maybe it was, she thought as she turned away again. If he'd been a kinder man he would have accepted her hand of friendship and her pathetic need to maintain contact with him would not have driven her to walk here to post him silly little notes.

Then she would not have been standing here like a prime target for Carlo Carlucci to amuse himself with—again.

Easy, he'd called her. And she flinched, ashamed of herself—disgusted with him for playing with her as if she was a toy.

Well, she wasn't anyone's toy. She wasn't *easy* either—and it was about time that she remembered that! Her chin came up, her hazel eyes glazing over with contempt for the hateful Carlo Carlucci. What was he after all but just one man among many that believed all women were fair prey?

She began to walk, feeling better now she'd managed to snatch her shaken pride back from the brink.

Villa Batiste came into view, its white marble walls drenched in the coral warmth of the late-afternoon sun. The contrast between it and Palazzo Gianni was so pronounced that Francesca pulled to a stop for a moment, struck by the sudden realisation that she did not like this beautiful place. It was all too neat, too shiny and pampered; even the elegant gardens had been groomed to within the tips of their hard edges.

But what the heck? It was a great place to throw a party, she decided, and with a lighter step she began walking up the long, straight driveway with its ceremonial guard of cedar-tree soldiers flanking her approach. She was just walking around the circular courtyard in front of the house when she saw Angelo come through the front door and a light came on inside her that quite simply lit her up. He was wearing jeans and a loose-fitting white sweatshirt and his hair shone golden in the sun.

She began to run to him, and he opened his arms and grinned as she raced up the shallow flight of steps. She fell into those open arms—and fell into his warm, familiar kiss. Oh, she loved—loved—loved this beautiful man, she thought happily.

'You've no *idea* how much I've missed you,' she sighed when the kiss eventually ended.

'I think I got the message,' he grinned.

It was then that she noticed the tiredness around his eyes and the hint of strain tugging at his mouth. 'Bad day?' she asked softly, running a gentle finger along a newly arrived groove at the corner of his mouth.

'Bad week,' he grimaced, then added with feeling, 'I never want to get on the wrong side of Carlo Carlucci again.'

Oh, Francesca could sympathise with that. Then she remembered to be annoyed with him for what he'd said to Carlo Carlucci and was just about to tackle him about it when the sound of a car horn grabbed their attention and the embrace was broken so they could turn to watch a minibus come hurtling up the drive.

She smiled in recognition, relaxing into the warmth of Angelo's circling arms as she watched the minibus pull to a stop at the bottom of the steps. Doors were flung open. People began piling out. Francesca's friends and work colleagues had arrived, having commandeered one of the company tour buses so they could travel here *en masse*. They were staying overnight in a hotel in the town but they'd stopped here first to drop off Sonya, who, like Bianca and several others, had had to work today or she would have travelled here with Francesca and Angelo's parents.

There were fifteen people in all, and every one of them had eyes round like saucers as they scanned the magnificence of Villa Batiste, making suitably impressed comments to each other and tossing teasing ones at Francesca and Angelo.

Sonya was the last one to climb out of the bus. She was wearing a simple white shift-dress that clung to her slender figure and left a good portion of her long legs on show. As she took her time turning a full circle to view her surroundings the late-afternoon sun placed a pale copper gloss on her flaxen hair. She really was beautiful. Everyone said so—except Angelo. He said that her looks were spoiled by her own vanity. That too many compliments had given her a hard edge. The fact that Sonya held much the same views on Angelo was a classic sign that they were two people whose strong characters just did not mix.

When Sonya finally lifted that delicate, heart-shaped face to look at them, Francesca felt an instant pang of irritable despair as she read the sardonic expression in her wide-spaced baby-blue eyes because she knew Sonya was mocking the overt display of wealth here.

Angelo must have seen it too because his arms tightened around her and he uttered something nasty beneath his breath.

'Oh, wow, this place is amazing!' one of the others exclaimed. 'Why isn't it on our tour list?'

'Don't let my mother hear you say that,' Angelo responded drily. 'She will send you all back the way you have come before you have a chance to do more than gasp.'

Group laughter rippled into the late-afternoon sunlight. One of the many things Francesca loved about Angelo was his willingness to send up. He might be a fully paid-up member of Rome's wealthy set but he had never allowed that to tarnish his attitude to her less advantaged friends. He was easy-going and warm and generous. He liked to be liked.

Unlike someone Francesca knew who did not give a care what anyone thought of him. He simply strolled through his life, upsetting anyone he wanted to upset and to heck with the consequences. But then, Carlo Carlucci was a fully paid-up member of the very *upper* echelons of Rome's wealthy set. A cut above the rest in other words—a very large cut.

Oh, stop thinking about him, she told herself crossly and was glad to have her thoughts diverted when a mass migration back into the minibus began to take place. Angelo strode down the steps to take Sonya's overnight bag for her, and the two exchanged stiff if polite words then came to join Francesca to wave the minibus off.

A silence fell. Sonya was pretending a deep interest in the garden while Angelo became engrossed in his shoes. Standing between them, Francesca glanced from one to the other then uttered a heavy sigh. She'd never managed to find out exactly what it was that had started hostilities between the two of them but she did know that it was getting worse.

Angelo shifted, his square chin rising. 'Shall we go in?' he said politely then he turned and strode into the house with Sonya's bag. The atmosphere cloyed as they followed him into the sheer grandeur of the green and white marble reception hall and walked together up the imposing curve of the white marble staircase. Pushing open a door to one of the bedroom suites, Angelo stood back to allow the two women to enter a place fit for visiting royalty.

Sonya walked forward and stood with her back to them. Angelo remained standing stiffly by the door. 'If I plead very hard, will you *please* be nice to each other for tonight?' Francesca burst out.

'Excuse me,' Angelo said. 'My father is expecting me in his study.' Then he left, closing the door behind him with a quiet click.

Sonya turned to look at Francesca. 'Don't blame me for that,' she said. 'I never did a single thing!'

'I know you didn't,' Francesca agreed with her. 'I apologise for him.'

'You don't have to do that,' Sonya said irritably. 'He's just…'

Mad at me, Francesca found herself finishing the sentence and then began to frown because she didn't understand why she would think like that unless…

It hit her then, just what this war between Sonya and Angelo was all about. 'It's the married man you're seeing,' she declared suddenly. 'Angelo knows who it is, doesn't he?'

To her grim satisfaction Sonya gasped out a choking response then spun away from her in a way that all but confirmed her accusation. Things suddenly began to fit. Their barbed comments to each other, the heated exchanges they had in quiet corners that lasted less than thirty seconds but always managed to destroy a pleasant atmosphere. And more relevant was that the hostilities had only started two weeks ago, which, according to Bianca, was when Sonya's new affair began. Two weeks ago Angelo had asked her to marry him. When she said yes, he'd arranged a celebration dinner at one of his favourite restaurants. It was the first time that Sonya had come into contact with Angelo's family. She cast her mind back, searching that sea of new faces, hunting out the married ones and trying to decide which one might be willing to cheat on his wife.

How did I miss all of this before? she asked herself. But she knew how. She had spent the last two weeks so engrossed in her love for Angelo that she hadn't been able to see anything beyond it.

But there was worse to come as yet another thought hit. 'He's going to be here tonight, isn't he?' she challenged. 'He'll be coming here with his wife and you're going to think you can sneak off with him somewhere for a little while!'

'That's so much rubbish,' Sonya denied.

No, it wasn't. 'I know you, Sonya,' she said. 'I know how common sense shoots right out of the window when a new man comes into your life.'

'You sound like my mother again.'

She did, Francesca acknowledged and this time didn't care. 'Angelo is worried that you're both going to risk causing a scene tonight. I bet he even asked you both not to come.'

'You're so way off the mark, it's sad to listen to you.' Sonya bent to collect her bag.

'Then *why* is Angelo mad at you?' she demanded outright.

Sonya didn't answer but just walked across the room and threw open the first door that she came to. The fact that it happened to be the bathroom was due to luck more than anything, but as she went to slam the door shut so she didn't have to have this discussion, Francesca got in one final plea.

'Promise me you won't do anything stupid tonight, *cara*,' she begged anxiously. 'I need your assurance—please.'

For a moment she thought Sonya was going to go on protesting her innocence, then it was as if all the fight just trickled out of her and she released a heavy sigh. 'So long as you promise to keep Angelo away from me,' she bartered. 'And *don't* try to get out of me who the man is!'

The bathroom door swung shut. Francesca winced as she turned back to the main door. She was just stepping out onto the landing when she heard the sound of raised voices echoing in the hall below. She paused, her heart beginning to beat faster when she recognised Angelo's angry tones.

'Do you think I am a fool? Of course I am not going to risk everything now! Your business is safe, Papa, take my word for it,' he said bitterly. 'And don't forget which of us is paying the price for it!'

Angelo's father spoke then but she couldn't hear what he was saying because he wasn't as angry as his son. Then a door closed and she could hear nothing else, but she was left wondering if the Batiste business was in trouble.

Had Carlo Carlucci lived up to Alessandro Batiste's worst fears and threatened to remove his business and take it else-where?

The wretched man was beginning to cast a very long shadow over almost everything that was important in her life, she mused grimly as she stepped into her own room next to Sonya's and closed the door. If *he* was a married man she would have to start wondering if he was Sonya's new lover! Sonya's reed-slender beauty being most defi-nitely his type!

And on that truly caustic note she took herself off to the

bathroom to indulge in a long, hot, tension-relieving soak before she had to present herself downstairs to help welcome the other guests that Angelo's parents had invited to stay overnight at the villa.

'I promised myself I wasn't going to do this.' She frowned at the mirror.

'Do what?' Sonya was standing behind her, busily fixing a beaded comb into the twisted knot she'd fashioned with Francesca's hair that now felt as if it had left her creamy shoulders and neck vulnerably exposed.

'Buy something that moulded.'

She was no raving beauty and had never pretended otherwise to herself. She might be tall and slender with passably attractive legs, but she possessed curves—old-fashioned curves like a waist and hips and full, firm breasts that sort of pouted whatever she wore. They were doing it now, pushing up above the straight edge of the bodice as if they were trying to escape.

'Oh, dear,' she sighed, and with a shimmy and a tug tried to pull the bodice up a bit.

'You're too critical of yourself,' Sonya mumbled from behind her. 'Have you any idea how many women shell out thousands to get C cups like yours?

'They can have mine for free,' Francesca muttered.

She'd gone shopping for classic black sophistication that would put her on a par with her super-elegant guests tonight and come back with this sultry dark red creation that was supposed to skim not cling to all those places she did not want to accentuate. The silk organza skirt was its saving grace with its ankle-length handkerchief edge. It was singularly the most expensive item of clothing she had ever bought, and, 'I look like a lush.'

'Idiot,' Sonya chided. 'You look like the lovely belle at your own ball, which is how it should be.' She finished securing the hair comb then stepped back to study the over-all look. 'Gosh, that colour suits you.'

'It reminded me of the ruby setting in my ring,' she explained, which was why she'd bought it instead of nice, safe black. 'Do you think Angelo will like it?'

'I think Angelo will adore it,' Sonya replied without a single hint of her usual caustic spoiling her tone. Then she turned away to pick up the fine chiffon scarf that came with the dress. 'Here, let's drape this around your shoulders just so and—presto, we have a princess.'

'We have an overdressed Barbie doll.'

'No.' Sonya appeared beside her in the mirror wearing a short skimpy blue satin slip dress that matched the colour of her eyes. '*I'm* the Barbie doll around here, *cara*,' she pronounced. 'Complete with twenty-four-inch spiked shoes.'

They both fell into a fit of the giggles, which was nice because they hadn't done much laughing recently—not since Sonya and Angelo fell out. 'I'm going to miss having you around when I'm married,' Francesca confided softly once they'd both calmed down again.

There was a silence—a stillness, both short, both tight. Then Sonya uttered a different kind of laugh. 'You must be joking. You'll be too busy doing something else to miss me.'

She was talking about making love but the moment that Francesca tried to visualise that Rubicon moment all she saw was a deeply sardonic dark, handsome face. It shook her so badly that she actually gasped.

'What?' Sonya demanded sharply, staring at her suddenly whitened face.

'Nothing,' she dismissed because how could she confess to Sonya what she had just seen? She would laugh—and why not? To her it would be one in the eye to her favourite enemy, Angelo, to learn that another man could arouse hot visions of lust inside his sex-shy fiancée.

She frowned again. It was beginning to worry her that she could feel like this about another man when she was about to commit herself to Angelo.

There was a knock at the door then. Sonya went to answer it. It was Angelo, come to escort Francesca downstairs. With a stiff smile and a mumbled, 'See you down there,' Sonya left them alone, pulling the door shut behind her as Francesca was turning from the mirror.

The moment she looked at him all her worries faded. He was wearing a formal black dinner suit and bow-tie and he looked so handsome that she felt herself melting inside. He was smiling at her, he was warm, he was all sunlight not mocking darkness. I'm just suffering from pre-betrothal nerves, she told herself and found her own smile when he sighed and said, '*Ah, bella—bella, mi amore.* You take my breath away.'

And that was all that she wanted, she told herself as she moved towards him. She wanted to take Angelo's breath away. She wanted to bask in the warmth of his love.

Which was exactly what she did for the next few hours, as the villa slowly filled with people and Angelo rarely left her side. The official announcement of their engagement was to take place at midnight and until then everyone was encouraged to sample the banquet buffet laid out in one of the grand salons or dance to the music provided by a group of live musicians in another grand salon. By ten the villa was throbbing with music and laughter and the more elegant hum of conversation.

She noted Carlo Carlucci's arrival at around ten o'clock. Who didn't note it? she thought sourly as she watched surreptitiously the way he drew people to him without him having to do more than stand by the main salon doors. He'd arrived without the usual beauty hanging on his arm, which surprised her. And he also made no effort to come anywhere near her, which was also a surprise since it wasn't very polite of him to keep his distance.

But it was an even bigger relief. She didn't want him using one of his mocking smiles on her, or worse—letting it drop that they'd met by accident a couple of times and exposing the fact that she hadn't mentioned those meetings to Angelo.

She would do, she promised herself. Tomorrow maybe when this was all over. But for now she was happy—happy—happy again and wanted to keep it that way.

Sonya, she saw, was behaving herself and sticking close to their own friends and work colleagues. If her new lover was here tonight—and Francesca was certain that he was here somewhere—she couldn't tell from Sonya's manner who the man was.

And foolishly she relaxed enough to drop her watchful guard on her friend. She was too busy being passed from one partner to another to be whirled beneath glittering crystal chandeliers. She was showered with beautiful compliments and teased and flirted with as only the Italians could do with such stylish panache. It was such a novelty to be the centre of everyone's attention like this that she began to feel intoxicated by it—or was it the champagne?

Each time she paused for breath someone placed a long, fluted glass in her fingers and bid her a toast that demanded she sip. Her cheeks had discovered a permanent rosy hue and her eyes sparkled beneath the overhead lights. Angelo was being treated to the same kind of attention. They would whirl by each other occasionally and share a laughing comment, but that was all they were allowed.

It was as if there was a conspiracy afoot to keep the two lovers apart until the bewitching hour and when she challenged one of her partners with the suspicion he laughed and whirled her away. No one would know from observing this glitter-bright gaiety that the whole thing was about to shatter with the same spectacular force you would get if one of the huge chandeliers suddenly dropped to the floor.

Francesca was taking a moment to catch her breath when

she happened to see Sonya quietly slipping away behind one of the gold-embossed curtains that had been drawn across a wall of French windows that led outside. Her antennae began to sing, sending her eyes flickering quickly around the room to see if anyone was going to follow her out.

It had to be her misfortune that her eyes clashed with those belonging to Carlo Carlucci. He was still holding court by the salon doors, standing with his dark head slightly tilted to one side as he listened to whatever the person with him was saying to him.

But his dark eyes were fixed on her.

That prickling sensation arrived, scoring tight *frissons* down her back, and she quickly dragged her eyes away from him and began weaving her way towards the French windows, determined to put a stop to the clandestine meeting she was now absolutely certain Sonya had arranged.

Sonya had left one of the doors slightly ajar. Slipping quietly through the gap, she walked across the wide marble terrace towards the stone balustrade beyond which the garden began to drop in a series of stylised tiers. It was cold out here, the late-spring chill in the air sending her hands up to rub at her bare arms as she paused to scan the darkened gardens in search of Sonya and her new man.

She heard them before she saw them, her slender body twisting towards the sound of scuffling feet and hushed voices filtering up from the terrace below. They were standing by the lower balustrade, and she was surprised to see that it was Angelo who was gripping one of Sonya's arms while she was trying to tug herself free.

'Let go of me!' she heard Sonya hiss out angrily.

'No,' Angelo rasped. 'I won't let you ruin this, Sonya—'

'I'm still going to tell her,' Sonya lashed back. 'She deserves to know the truth before this charade goes any further. I will be doing her a favour.'

She was threatening to confess her affair to her lover's wife! Oh, dear God, Francesca thought. She couldn't let her do that! She was about to move towards the steps to go down there to add her own pleas to Angelo's—when Angelo's harsh reply stalled her feet.

'You think she will be grateful to you for your big confession, heh, *cara*? Do you think she will fall on your neck and forgive you, her closest friend, for sleeping with me, the man she is heart and soul in love with...?'

And that was the point where everything shattered, sprinkling around her like fine crystal shards that lacerated her flesh as they fell.

CHAPTER FOUR

FRANCESCA began to shake so badly she could barely stay upright, even her heart trembling, clawing at the walls of her chest as if it was trying to escape from what she was being made to face. She struggled to believe it, didn't *want* to believe it. She even closed her eyes and replayed Angelo's words inside her head in a silly, stupid, desperate attempt to find out where she had misunderstood what he'd said.

But there was no misunderstanding, Sonya's next shrill claim made it too sickeningly clear. 'You don't want her! You don't even like her that much!'

'What I want and I what I am to have are two different issues.'

'Money,' Sonya sliced at him. 'As if the Batistes haven't got enough of it locked up in this place, you're willing to marry a woman you have no feelings for just to lay your hands on the Gianni fortune! It's disgusting. '

'And none of your damn business,' Angelo rasped.

'While you can't keep your hands off me, it's my damn business.'

There was a groan—an agonised groan that brought Francesca's eyelids flickering upwards to watch as Angelo pulled Sonya against him then buried his mouth in her throat. 'I cannot get you out of my head,' he muttered. 'I close my eyes and all I see is you, naked, on top of me.'

'When your little heiress is naked on top of you, will you close your eyes and think of me then?'

The vile taunt brought Angelo's head up, set his hands moving in a tense, urgent, restless sweep over Sonya's slippery blue satin dress. 'Yes,' he said thickly.

Francesca swayed, her whole world tilting sideways as if it was trying to tip her off. A pair of arms came around her from behind and covered her shivering arms where they still folded like clamps across her front. Long brown fingers closed over her icy fingers, a solid male torso became a supporting wall to her trembling back. A dark head lowered, a pair of lips came to rest on her ear.

'Heard enough?' Carlo asked in a soft, rough voice that scraped over her cold flesh like sand across silk.

She wasn't even surprised that it was him who was holding her. In some mad, tortuous way it seemed fitting that he would be the one to witness this—as if the two of them had been building towards this devastating moment for days.

She was about to attempt a nod in answer to his question when Angelo uttered a thick groan and took fierce possession of Sonya's lips. Sonya didn't even try to stop him. The way they kissed, open-mouthed, deep and frantic, their two blond heads locked together. The way they touched, hands moving over each other in hot, tight, convulsive movements that stripped clean to the bone any lingering doubts she might have had that they'd done this many times before. A long, silken thigh was exposed to the hip bone, a small, pale breast was uncovered to receive the hungry clamp of Angelo's mouth. It only took eyes to see that Sonya was wearing nothing at all beneath the skimpy scrap of silk. She'd come prepared for this, despite all the angry threats and protests she'd just uttered, she'd had no intention of missing out on the sex.

Sickened, Francesca began to shudder. Carlo responded with a swiftness that caught her breath. The soft hiss of his anger stung her icy, quivering face as he twisted her around then tugged her against him and held her there for a moment while she shivered and shook.

Then Angelo's voice came, raw with pleasure. 'Yes, do that again,' he groaned.

For a horrible moment Francesca thought she was going to faint. Carlo Carlucci must have thought so too because the next thing she knew one of his arms had hit the backs of her knees and she was being lifted off the ground.

'I'm all right,' she choked.

His lips arrived at her ear again to utter the harsh rasp, 'Be quiet or they will hear you.'

The very thought of that happening had her curling into him. He started moving, long, swift strides taking them the full length of that side of the villa. A stunning silence arrived as they turned the corner and it was only then Francesca realised that the whole ugly thing had taken place to a background of music and laughter filtering out from the house.

He kept on going further and further down this wing, which housed the more private apartments that were not being used for the party tonight. All the windows were shrouded in darkness, the only light coming from the hazed moon hanging in the night sky. He pulled to a stop beside yet another set of French doors. The villa was ringed with them; elegantly styled and evenly spaced, they gave every room on the ground floor its own access onto the wide terraces that flanked all four sides of the house.

She felt tensile muscles flex as he reached down to try a handle. A door slid open and he swung her inside. It was dark in here too, but she did manage to register that he'd brought her to Mr Batiste's private study with its heavy, dark pieces of furniture that didn't blend in with the rest of the house.

Then she was being dumped on a leather chair by the fireplace with logs neatly laid in the grate ready to light. Still shivering, she instantly wrapped her arms back round her body as Carlo moved to close the door they'd just used. She heard a key turn and quivered, though she didn't know why she did. Then he was moving swiftly in the other direction and a second later another key turned in the door leading out to the hall.

'Don't,' she said when she saw him raise a hand towards the light switch.

The hand dropped to his side and she tried to relax some of the screaming tension from her body. It didn't happen. Too many muscles had locked and knotted and she'd never felt so cold in her entire life.

Still without comment he began to move again. He was nothing more than a shifting shadow in the darkness, and right now she was happy to keep him like that. She didn't want to see his face—she didn't want him to look into her own. She felt stripped and raped and bruised and battered.

This time she heard the chink of glass on glass.

Angelo and Sonya—Sonya and Angelo. Her eyes drifted shut as that dreadful little litany began playing itself over and over inside her head alongside frame-by-frame images of what she had just seen.

The open-mouthed kiss that devoured greedily, the slippery blue satin that was so willing to slide away from a silken thigh and hip. She heard the gasps, the groans of passionate agony, and felt sick to her stomach because all she'd ever got was quietly, calmly—briefly wrapped in a light-hearted affection, not the raging fires and animal lust.

What a perfectly choreographed act they'd put on for her benefit, she thought painfully. What a smooth blinding mask they'd pulled over her eyes as they snipped and sniped at each other the way that they had.

And what a sick—sick joke the two of them had been enjoying at her expense.

Humiliation poured through her bloodstream, the power of it grinding her bruised heart against her ribs. Dragging up her eyelids, she stared down at her dress. Angelo had not felt compelled to drag down this bodice and lay bare one of her breasts. He'd never once so much as stroked her thigh. The light touches she'd received that she'd believed were offered with love and tenderness and respect now became touches of idle contempt wrapped up in calculation and necessity.

He'd intended to marry her and take her to bed only when he had to do it and even then he was going to impose

Sonya's sylph-like image over her to help him get through the ordeal.

She quivered again, despising him for doing this to her—despising herself for being so gullible and blind.

A sound reached into her consciousness—people laughing as they walked past the closed study door. The party, she remembered. Her engagement party. Hers and Angelo's.

The Gianni heiress and the fortune-hunter, she then thought bitterly.

But she was no heiress. There was no fortune to be had if she was. And she could not understand why Angelo could believe otherwise when she'd already told him the hard truth about her connection to the Gianni name.

'Here, drink some of this…'

She hadn't realised her eyes had closed again until she was forced to open them. The dark shadow was squatting in front of her, she realised, though she hadn't noticed him arrive there. Only he wasn't quite a dark shadow any more because her eyes had adjusted to the darkness. So she could see the way he was studying her narrowly, the way he was holding his mouth thin and flat. The bright white of his shirt stood out, casting reflected light along the grim set of his chiselled jaw bone as he placed the rim of a glass to her mouth. She sipped without protest. The brandy trickled across her tongue and she forced herself to swallow, leaving warm vapours behind in her mouth.

He sipped too. She watched with unblinking absorption as he lifted the glass away from her lips to place it against his own. His throat moved as he swallowed, shifting the butterfly collar to his shirt. He held the glass between long brown fingers while her own pale fingers still clutched at her arms, her nails scoring crescents into the icy bare skin.

'H-how much did you overhear?' she whispered unsteadily.

For a moment she thought he wasn't going to answer, his mouth compressing. Then, 'Most if it,' he admitted, and rose to his full height.

She looked away from him—at the logs piled in the grate—on a sinking sense of dismay that robbed a bit more of her ravaged pride. This tall, dark, sophisticated man of Rome had stood there in the background witnessing the brutal murder of everything she cared about.

She felt stripped bare again and flayed this time.

'Why were you out there?' No one else had been out there—or at least she hoped no one else had been there!

The laughter came again, echoing around the marble hallway and sounding cruelly mocking to her oversensitised ears. It was then that a sudden thought hit that was so horrible it feathered her breathing. How many of those people out there knew the real motives behind Angelo's engagement to her? Did they all know? Did all her friends know about Sonya's affair with Angelo?

Had Carlo Carlucci known it all even before he stepped outside tonight? Her breath feathered again as she shifted her gaze back to his tense profile.

'You weren't there by accident, were you?' she charged shakily. 'You suspected that something was going to happen so you followed me outside then s-stood there like some—s-sleazy voyeur—'

His dark head turned to lance her an amused look. 'You see me as sleazy?'

No, she didn't, but… 'Don't laugh at me!' she bit out painfully. 'None of this is funny!'

'You're right.' The laughter died. 'It isn't.'

The threat of tears came then. She dragged in a deep breath, fighting to stop them, fighting to keep her mind fixed on what had started her travelling along this thread. 'H-how much of it did you know before you followed me?'

Without answering her he turned abruptly and walked away, disappearing back into the shadows at the other end of the room as if the darkness could save him from having to offer a reply.

But she needed to know. 'How much?' she launched shrilly after him.

'All of it.'

The answer hit her like a blow. Her breasts heaved behind her crossed arms, and for a moment she felt dizzy again. Then she pulled herself together and asked the next wretched question burning a hole inside her head. 'And—everyone else out there?'

She heard the fresh chink of glass on glass before the words came, felt the angry tension in him as he poured another drink. 'Your true identity became an open secret within days of you meeting Angelo,' he told her. 'The fact that you were not announcing that you are the heiress to the huge Gianni fortune only helped to fuel the fires of intrigue and speculation as to why you wanted to play the ordinary working girl and keep your identity such a closed secret.'

'I'm not the Gianni heiress,' she denied. 'There is no fortune to be had.'

He laughed like a cynic. 'You are worth so much money, Francesca, *cara*, that the figure can make Rome's wealthiest blanch.'

Which was all so much rubbish her brows snapped together. 'Stupid rumour and speculation,' she dismissed. 'Bruno Gianni lives in a ruin. He has no money to leave to anyone, never mind a great-niece he won't even see!'

'Well, you're right about Bruno's money,' Carlo drawled as he strode back into view. 'But we're not talking about Bruno Gianni's money. We are talking about *Rinaldo* Gianni's money. Your grandfather,' he extended as if she needed that clarified, and bent to prise a set of cold fingers away from her arm so he could slot a fresh glass of brandy between them. 'The fortune is his,' he continued. 'Rinaldo left everything to you. Bruno only lives in the *palazzo* at your behest because it, like everything else, belongs to you—or it will do when you marry,' he then amended, 'a man from a good Italian family, I think is near as damn it to the official working of his will. The lot to be held in a trust to be solely administered by his surviving brother until you comply. Angelo thought he'd hit gold when he seduced you into falling in love with him,' he added. 'He's the real hero of the party tonight, *cara*. The man who pulled off the perfect coup.'

She was beginning to think she was dreaming all of this. 'I don't have a clue what you're talking about,' she said.

'I know.' He used that laugh again. 'And that is the real irony of it.'

He went to lean a shoulder against the mantel, pushed his hands into his trouser pockets then studied her ashen face as he continued.

'While everyone else thinks you're being intriguingly clever and infuriatingly devious, you are merely oblivious to it all. It took me weeks to suss you out,' he confessed as if that was some kind of shock in itself. 'You are not pretending to be the wide-eyed and beautiful, naïve innocent— you *are* her. And Bruno Gianni has a lot to answer for— which he will do when I get my hands round his wicked old throat.'

'You won't go near my uncle Bruno,' she muttered dimly, feeling swamped by words that didn't make any sense.

'What—protecting the hand that robs you, Francesca?' he mocked. 'What were you—ten years old when your grand-father died? For the last fourteen years he's been sitting on your inheritance and probably praying that you never show your face in Rome.'

'Stop it,' she jerked out. 'There's just been a dreadful misunderstanding, that's all!' she cried. 'Angelo knows the truth. He knows I'm—'

His hiss of impatience snapped her lips shut. 'Get real, Francesca,' he derided. 'You heard what that mercenary bas-tard said out there! To start trying to defend him is bloody pathetic! He wants your money,' he lanced down at her. 'He *needs* your money! Get that into your lovesick head and deal with it!'

He was angry—why was he angry? That was her prerog-ative! She was the one being used and abused and talked about as if she was some kind of juicy commodity!

'There is no money!' She launched herself to her feet to spit the denial at him. 'And what makes you any better than Angelo when you actually believe all that stuff you just threw at me?'

There was a glinting flash behind narrowed eyelids, a glimpse of angry white teeth. A hand snaked out and she released a choked cry as he clamped his fingers round her wrist.

'Don't compare me with Batiste—ever,' he bit out from between those white teeth.

'I w-wasn't...' The confused words disintegrated when she began trembling all over again, shocked by the sudden eruption of violence in him. His dark face had changed out of all recognition, the clenched bones, the narrowed eyes glinting with a danger she could actually taste. Her heart was pounding, her wrist hurting where he held it in a vice-like grip.

He hated Angelo, she realised—despised him with a ferocity that had turned him primitive.

She tugged at her wrist. He held it fast. The next thing she was drawing in a sharp breath when the other hand came up. She thought he was going to slap her. Her eyes widened as the cold sweat of fear broke out on her skin. 'No...' she husked.

And was dragged even deeper into the mud of confusion when he began carefully easing the brandy glass she had forgotten she was holding out of her clenched fingers and she realised with new horror that it was aimed to empty its contents into his face.

Not just his violence but her violence. Her head began to swim. She wasn't a violent person, so how had she reached the point of wanting to throw brandy into someone's face?

The glass was removed. The wrist released. She took it in her other hand and began absently rubbing it while her insides were so shaken up she had the hysterical impression she was going to fall into little pieces any minute.

'There is no money,' she repeated, trying desperately to cling to this one safe thread.

The hard angles in his face didn't soften, the eyes still glittered in the chiselled set of his face. And his voice when it came was like cold steel slicing through silk. 'Whether there is or there isn't money, is not actually the important issue—not when you manage to remember what your friend and Batiste were doing out there, that is…'

And just like that she was devastated, the steel-like thrust of his point cutting right to the core of everything because she *had* been concentrating on the money thing instead of what really mattered here.

She'd been used and betrayed by two people she loved most. Duped like a fool because she'd been too blinded by trust to see what was happening beneath her nose.

It all came crashing down again, coiling like a tight band around her aching chest, and fresh tears began to build in her throat.

The rows, the *passion* it required to generate so much hostility. Sonya's guilty looks, the lies that had tripped so defiantly from her tongue. Money had nothing to do with Sonya's part in her betrayal. She'd just wanted Angelo with a fever that had raged out of control. So she'd had him, because the wanting had been more powerful than her loyalty to a close friend!

And the money had nothing to do with the sexual part of Angelo's betrayal because he must have known he was putting everything at risk when he gave in to his desire for Sonya. For who else was more likely to confess all in a fit of conscience than the closest friend to his future wife?

His future wife. The one he would take to bed only when he had to.

Oh, dear God… 'I've got to get away from here,' she whispered on a sudden burst of panic and reeled away to take a couple of shaky steps towards the terrace doors.

Everything happened so fast then that she was thrown into shock. There was a muttered curse followed by two hands arriving at her waist and she was being lifted bodily off the floor, turned and dumped unceremoniously back to the floor then clamped to a hard male chest.

'What are you—?'

'Shut up,' he ground out furiously. 'Someone is coming.'

And she froze like a statue as she heard the sound of Angelo's voice calling her name from the terrace just outside their door. The door handle rattled. Her heart withered in her chest and her fingers went up to clutch at the lapels to Carlo Carlucci's dinner jacket.

'I don't want to see him,' she choked. And she didn't. She never wanted to set eyes on Angelo again!

'I locked the door,' his grim voice reminded her.

'He will see us through the glass.' She moved even closer to his superior framework as if trying to blend right into him.

His arms accommodated her, a hand gently curving round her slender nape, the other splaying across the low part of her back. 'He can't see you,' he murmured in husky reassurance. 'It's dark in here. I am wearing black and my back is to the window. If he sees anything it will be the dark outline of one of his male guests enjoying a snatched moment in his father's study with one of his female guests.'

'M-me,' she pointed out.

There was a short silence. Then he said cynically, 'Did you tell him about our two meetings, *cara*? How very loyal of you.'

The cold taunt brought her eyes up to clash with his. The guilty flush that mounted her cheeks said all she needed to say.

'Well—well,' he murmured. 'It seems to me that your whole life is built on dangerous secrets, *mi amore*.'

'I don't have *any* secrets,' she snapped. 'And there was nothing dangerous about our two brief meetings!' she added, frowning at the sudden quickening she felt in her pulse.

'Liar,' he drawled. 'We connected sexually. I don't know how you kept your hands off me.'

'How did you *ever* get to be so arrogant?' she gasped, staring at him.

'It took practice,' he replied, and the weird thing about this conversation was that it was so deadly serious without a hint of mockery to be heard! In fact she could see that frightening anger simmering in his eyes. 'You want to be thankful that I am attracted to you or you would be languishing somewhere in the Batiste garden, slowly dying from a broken heart by now.'

It was like being kicked when she was already lying in a battered heap on the ground. On a stifled choke she went to step away from him. Once again he showed his superior strength to keep her still.

'I hate you,' she choked.

He didn't bother to answer. She could feel the strength in his fingers where they pressed into her lower back and the very disturbing presence of his thumbs slowly circling against her stomach wall. Tiny senses began to stir in places she didn't want them to, low in her abdomen and in the tips of her breasts. It was mad; the whole crazy evening was turning her quietly insane. She hardly knew him, she certainly didn't like him yet here she was, standing in his arms, letting him tell her that she fancied going to bed with him!

The door handle rattled again. 'Who is in there?' Angelo's glass-muffled voice questioned impatiently.

'Persistent devil,' Carlo said. 'Perhaps we should give him a taste of his own medicine.'

Alarm stiffened her backbone. 'No!' was all she could get out before he lowered his dark head.

It was the sheer, heart-stopping shock of it that held her immobile, the unfamiliar touch of his mouth against hers. He was taller than Angelo, darker than Angelo, harder and stronger and more forceful than Angelo had ever been with her. Her startled lips were ruthlessly parted, and his tongue darted through the gap. A tight rush of sensation shot from her mouth to her breasts to low in her abdomen then poured like quicksilver down her legs.

She had never experienced anything like it. A shocked, disorientated whimper clawed at her throat as she was suddenly flung into alien territory, the heat, the intrusion, the flagrant intimacy of that invading tongue exploring the inner tissue of her mouth trapping her inside butterfly tremors of bemused response.

He pulled his head back, glinting her a dark-eyed puzzled frown, saw her wide-eyed startlement, the revealingly shocked tremor of her lips. 'Did Angelo sexually starve you into submission?' he uttered with an oddly strained laugh.

She just continued to stare at him, too befuddled to take in the question, and his eyes took on a hard light. He hissed something unrepeatable about Angelo then lowered his head again to return to where he'd left off. Only this time with more heat, more sensual purpose, and his hands joined in, lifting and crushing her into closer contact with his body and holding her there while he ravaged her mouth. She felt the burgeoning power of his passion pressing against her then her own body responded as that place between her thighs began to pulse then grow damp. Sensation was slithering everywhere, in her bloodstream, coiling round muscles to make them writhe into greater contact.

It was shocking, so basic and—and physical! Her crushed breasts swelling and stinging painfully as her nipples grew tight.

The door handle rattled. She jerked her head back against his restraining hand and their lips parted with a disconcerting pop. Electric wires had been attached to every extremity. She was breathless yet panting. Her tongue and lips felt swollen and hot. He was staring down at her with glinting black fixed eyes and a perfect stillness, his expression peculiarly...

She didn't know what his face was telling her. She only knew she'd just been somewhere very perilous and that she did not like it—but she did.

Sex, she called it. *Lust* said it better. She'd been kissed with hot and driving passion for the first time in her life by a man who was very good at it.

Heat hit her pale cheeks. She dragged her eyes away from him and became aware of the way the flat of her hands braced painfully against the solid wall of chest. Everything about him was solid, his shoulders, his arms, the bowl of his hips where she could feel the solid column of his—

'Let me go,' she demanded hazily.

He did the opposite, pressing her closer then lowering his head again to flick his tongue across her burning lips. She almost detonated on a ball of hot static. A helpless cry keened in her throat.

Footsteps sounded as Angelo moved away from the window, bringing Carlo alive with a jolt. His eyes lost that frightening expression, his brows pushing together on a frown. His grip on her tightened and Francesca found herself being lifted again, swung around then unceremoniously dumped in the chair she had used before.

The wretched brandy glass was slotted back between her fingers. 'Drink it this time,' she was tersely instructed as he turned away.

'I'm dizzy enough,' she thought and didn't realise she'd said it out loud until his grim response came back.

'Think how you're going to feel in about five minutes. Because that is how long it will take Angelo to walk through the other door.'

Feeling as if she'd been tossed from a storm into a maelstrom, she stared at the solid wooden door which lead out to the main hallway as if it were some brooding dark monster. 'You locked it,' she breathed shakily.

He was already striding over there. To her utter consternation he turned the key to unlock the door.

'What did you do that for?' she cried out in protest.

Ignoring her, he reached up to flick the light switch next. It was like being bombarded with hot shards of glass. She screwed her eyes shut on a shrill little whimper of agony then dragged them open again almost immediately because she needed to know what he was going to do next. He was already halfway back across the room and bending down to pick something up off the floor. She'd never seen such a change in anyone. His energy levels had shot from virtually somnolent to the other extreme.

The black dinner suit barely rippled as he straightened up again, the butterfly collar to his white dress shirt still looked as crisp as it probably had when he'd first put it on. His skin wore a warm olive sheen and his satiny black hair had the merest hint of a wave that she hadn't noticed before. His head was bent slightly, eyes hooded, those thick lashes hovering a breath away from his chiselled cheekbones. He was breathtakingly attractive and his mouth wore the bloom of their recent kiss.

Fire pooled between her thighs again and she wrenched her eyes away from him. Everything about him was suddenly so physical, so—sexual!

Oh, dear, she groaned inwardly. What's happening to me?

Lifting up the glass, she took a large gulp at the brandy. Why not get drunk? she decided wildly. It had to be a better option to feeling like this.

He arrived in front of her, making her jump nervously when he bent to use one hand to take the glass from her so he could take his turn with the drink, while the other hand pulled her to her feet. She felt like a puppet—*this* man's puppet! He kept pulling and pushing her, picking her up, putting her down and *kissing* her.

Oh, dear, she thought again as her insides went haywire. 'No,' she husked in muffled protest.

'No what?' he asked, discarding the glass.

But she'd already forgotten what when he proceeded to hook long fingers beneath the lip of her bodice as if he had every right to touch her like this!

'What are you doing?' she choked out in protest as she felt the smooth backs of his nails stroke her flesh.

His answer was a demonstration. Coolly and very proficiently he gave a tug that resettled the dark fabric across the thrust of her breasts. Glancing down, she gave a gasp of horror when she realised how close she must have been to revealing too much flesh.

Like Sonya.

Like Sonya… Her eyes closed on the next dizzying wave to hit her as reality came crashing back.

He moved his attention elsewhere then, throwing her into a deeper state of confusion when he proceeded to tidy her tumbled hair. She hadn't even realised the knot had come undone.

'Now listen,' he said. 'We haven't got much time for this so you are going to have to make some quick decisions as to what happens next,' he said quietly, deciding to organise her wrecked life for her now, she noted dully.

'Lock the door again.' That was a decision.

She watched as his mouth compressed. 'The way I see it, you have several choices. You can turn a blind eye to what you saw and continue with tonight as if nothing has happened…' She winced at the word *blind*. 'Or you can brave it out and go out there of your own volition to announce that you're calling off the engagement and why you are.'

Either way she looked the fool. 'Great choices,' she muttered.

'I haven't finished yet,' he chided. 'If you really feel you can't bear to face him then we can leave through the French windows right now, before he gets here, climb into my car and just disappear.'

She glared at his chest and grimly added coward to fool and shrew.

He was using her hair comb to tame the thick silken swathe into some semblance of tidiness, surprising her with the efficiency he used to secure her hair in yet another neat twist. And her scalp was beginning to tingle—with pleasure. She couldn't bear it. It was all just too much.

'Please stop it, Carlo,' she breathed out anxiously.

'You do know my name, then,' he said lightly and she lifted her eyelids to show him dark pools of agony.

'Please lock the door again,' she pleaded. 'I'm not ready to cope with him!'

His fingers dropped to cup her shoulders, his eyes suddenly sober and dark. 'It is midnight, Francesca,' he informed her very gently.

Midnight. The witching hour. The time her engagement to Angelo was to be formally announced. Her gaze flicked the room as if a hundred glossy people were already standing here watching and waiting to bear witness as Angelo claimed his mighty prize.

She shuddered in dismay as the full weight of his betrayal returned like a flood. The hands on her shoulders moved in reflex response. 'Don't cry,' he said brusquely. 'He doesn't deserve your tears.'

She knew that, but it didn't stop what was beginning to break up inside. 'What am I going to do?' she whispered tragically.

His hands moved again, coming to frame her face so he could tilt it up to receive his next warm kiss. When she responded with a small sob he caught the sound with the lick of his tongue. Each stifled sob after it was gently robbed from her; in between he placed words, low, dark, seductive words that made her want to cling.

'Leave it to me,' he said. 'I will deal with it. Trust me to get you through this.'

'But why should you want to?' she asked, realising it was a question she should have asked a whole lot sooner than this. 'Why should it interest you at all?'

His answering smile was the cynical one. 'Come on, Francesca, the answer to that one must be perfectly clear,' he mocked as he moved one of his long thumbs to send it on a sweep of her now pulsing not quivering mouth. 'I want you for myself,' he told her grimly. 'Therefore I will do what it takes to get you.'

Then he was lowering his mouth again to show how

much he wanted her with yet another full-blooded mind-blowing kiss.

Everything he did now was laced with intimacy. Every touch, every look, every small gesture was staking claim. And the worst of it was that she let him. She felt so vulnerable and weak and drawn to his passion that she had a terrible suspicion he could spread her out on the desk across the room and have his way with her and she wouldn't try to stop him.

It was a dreadful admission. It shocked and appalled her but didn't make her pull away from him. Where was her pride, her dignity?

Not where her mouth was anyway. It clung and encouraged, like her fingers where they lifted and clung to his nape, smoothing, stroking, and her hips as they arched into the masculine bowl of his. And the whole hot, sensuous embrace was so slow and deep and intoxicatingly rousing, she moved with it, soaked in it, and didn't even hear the door flying open until a stunned voice rasped, 'What the hell do you think you are doing?'

CHAPTER FIVE

SHOCK wired her up to a live cable. She felt its electric fingers *frisson* her skin. On a choked gasp she tried to break free but Carlo was in no hurry to let that happen. He took his time easing the kiss, lingering long enough for Angelo to be in no doubt as to what he was witnessing here.

'As you can see, a great deal is going on,' he then murmured with smooth, slick—diabolical composure. And he said it without moving his eyes from Francesca's hot, kissed-hazed, dismayed face. He even dared to compound on his statement by shaping yet another warm, excruciatingly possessive kiss to her gaping mouth.

'Leave her alone!' Angelo bit out hoarsely. 'Francesca— come over here. I can't believe that you are doing this with him while everyone out there is waiting for our announcement!'

That last part really said it all, Francesca thought heavily. For here she stood, caught red-handedly wrapped in a passionate embrace with another man, and all Angelo could think about was getting his ring on her finger.

My God, that hurt.

'There will be no announcement,' Carlo declared smoothly. 'Francesca doesn't want you any more. You are out, *amico,* and I am in. You may announce that if you wish.'

It was an unbelievably cut-throat, throwaway comment, and Francesca could only stare up at the smooth, challenging face.

'I told you I would deal with it,' Carlo reminded her gently then placed a finger beneath her chin and calmly shut her still gaping mouth.

Angelo seemed incapable of saying anything. She could feel his confusion, his blank, bubbling bewilderment. She turned her head to look at him. He was standing two strides into the room with the door swinging wide open so he was framed by glaring white marble from the hall beyond. People were milling about, moving to or from one of the many rooms that had been opened up for tonight's party. Some halted and stared when they saw the little trio standing in Alessandro Batiste's study, making her aware suddenly of other things like the way her slender arms were still coiled around Carlo's neck and the front of her body resting intimately against his.

Culpable heat flooded up her throat and into her cheeks. 'Close the door,' she breathed on a stifled whisper.

Angelo's blue eyes flared to life and he spun about to see for himself the way they were being stared at. His arm shot out and the door slammed into its housing then he was twisting back to them again to pin her with a furious look.

'Explain to me what the hell you think you are doing with him,' he gritted.

It was like looking at a complete stranger. Nothing about him was familiar to her any more. His smooth golden features that had once looked beautiful to her now looked hard and selfish. The glitter in his eyes one of mercenary greed not tender possessiveness. How could she have missed all of that? she wondered painfully. Everything about him, from the contrived streaks in his tawny blond hair to the angrily petulant curl to his mouth, bore no resemblance to the man she'd thought she loved. An ache throbbed in her stomach; she had never felt so deceived—by herself. Blinded by smooth, deliberate lies and a pitiable desire to be loved.

A pair of hands slid around her waist. She looked back at Carlo and saw hardness and toughness and a strength of will in his face that promised to devour her if she let it. But she also saw truth. He was hiding nothing, pretending nothing. I want you, he'd said, nothing more—nothing less than that. But at least it was honest.

'Tell him, *cara*,' he prompted softly.

Her breasts heaved on a tense little breath and she looked back at Angelo. 'I'm not going to marry you,' she announced obediently then was shocked by how easily the words came out. 'You don't love me. You never even tried to.'

Then she looked back at Carlo. He didn't love her but at least he didn't say that he did. He kissed her gently. Maybe he could sense the aching threat of tears still working in her throat.

'Will you stop kissing her like that?' Angelo rasped out. 'Francesca—*amore*,' he pleaded huskily, 'of course I love you. How could you think I do not?'

A picture of an all-consuming open-mouthed kiss and an urgent hand sliding blue silk away from a slender thigh closed her eyes on a wave of thick anguish. She heard the sound of shrill words declaring, *You don't want her! You don't even like her that much!* echoing their bitter poison into her head.

'Listen,' Angelo planted into the swirling mists of that fading image, 'if this is a case of pre-engagement panic, Francesca, I can understand that. Come to me,' he urged. 'We will go somewhere private so we can talk about it...'

He was very good, Francesca acknowledged and even felt herself start to tremble inside because she was hearing that other Angelo again, the quiet and tender one she'd fallen in love with. Maybe they should discuss this without a third-party witness. Maybe she—

'Careful, *amore*,' a soft voice cautioned. 'Seduction can take many formats.'

He was right. She was being seduced by Angelo's tender charm again. How easy she must have made it all for him, she thought with a self-deprecating dismay that sent her swaying closer to this tall, dark man who was her only truly honest support right now because she certainly could not rely on herself!

Her mouth accidentally brushed the cleft in his chin, sending tight tingles of awareness skittering across her skin. She sucked in a soft gasp, shocked at how sensitised she had become to everything about him. His voice, his touch, she could even taste him—drew greedily on his subtle male scent.

Anger roared at her from across the room. *'Puttana!'*

She blinked, too dazed and disorientated by what she was feeling to really take the retort in, and she turned her head to find herself facing a man pulsing with biting contempt for her. The change from bewildered and pleading lover to this was startling. Golden eyes were flashing silver steel. A dark flush had mounted his skin. His teeth were showing, bared as if he were a riled wolf preparing to pounce.

Carlo had turned his head also. In the throes of all of this hostility it struck her that it was the first time he had bothered to look at Angelo. 'Be very careful whom you insult,' he warned with a soft-voiced snarl. 'Or I might decide to bring your house tumbling down like the flimsy pack of cards it is.'

And Francesca's skin began to prickle because if Angelo was a wolf then he was a mere puppy compared to this very dangerous man. Seeming to recognise that, Angelo instantly backed down, an unsteady sigh hissing from his lips as he ran a shaking set of fingers through his hair. He was floundering in a brain-numbing state of shock, she saw, and knew exactly what it felt like.

'But she can't to do this to me,' Angelo groaned out unsteadily.

'She can and she is.' It was so cold and brutal that she shivered, bringing his attention back to her again. Long fingers gently crushed silk chiffon against the sensitive skin at her waist as he lowered his head to brush his lips across the frown-creased bridge of her nose.

There was a sound of disgust as Angelo threw his back to them.

The door flew open. 'Angelo—Francesca, what are you doing in here? Your guests are…'

The words were cut off when she saw Carlo, her eyelashes flickering when she took in the scene. Angelina Batiste was blond and golden like Angelo but unlike Angelo it didn't take her more than a few seconds to understand what was really happening here and her face became a perfectly blank page.

'Leave us, Madre,' Angelo bit at her. 'I am dealing with this.'

But his mother was not going to leave. She was too busy seeing a terrible scandal staring her in the face and surprised everyone by turning on her son.

'What have you done?' she demanded accusingly.

'I've done nothing,' he growled, sounding like the puppy wolf again. 'Look to them for your culprits.' He tossed a hand out. 'The way they cannot stop kissing each other speaks for itself.'

'At least we do it with a lot more *finesse* than you were using on Francesca's flatmate, *amico*. And we sought privacy, not the garden, where anyone who wanted to could view your technique…'

Francesca closed her eyes as the world swayed at this next stark revelation. For a moment she thought she was going to faint. Angelina Batiste almost choked on the shocked gasp that rose in her throat.

Opening her eyes again, she saw Angelo had spun round to stare at them. He looked shattered. He'd had the high ground ripped from beneath him by a man with a lethal penchant for ruthlessness. It left him with no argument to pursue, nothing for him to say in his own defence.

He tried though, eyelashes flickering as he moved his stunned eyes to his mother's shock-whitened face then on to look at Francesca. *'Cara…'* he murmured in a huskily pleading, unsteady tone. 'For goodness' sake, don't listen to him. What he's implying isn't true.'

'Perhaps I should have explained that we *both* observed your lack of finesse,' Carlo inserted.

Angelo went white then an angry red. '*Bastardo!* Shut up!' he launched at Carlo. 'This has nothing to do with you!'

His mother jumped. Francesca blinked. Angelo took a step towards her. 'Listen to me,' he said urgently. 'What you saw tonight was a moment of madness. Your friend— she threw herself at me. She—'

A shrill gasp came from the doorway. None of them had noticed that it had been left open when Mrs Batiste came into the room. Angelo swung round—they all swivelled their eyes to find Sonya standing there with her beautiful face a study of icy anger and burning guilt.

'You lying son of a bitch,' she hissed at Angelo, causing his mother to stiffen in personal offence. 'We've been sleeping together for weeks!'

He was being attacked from all angles. He responded to that with violence. One of his arms came up and for a horrible second Francesca thought he was going to slap Sonya's face. His mother must have thought so too because she darted forward and in a mad scramble she took hold of Sonya's arm and hustled her from the room. Angelo's arm diverted to grab the door. It slammed into its housing again.

Silent hit. Singing in the turbulent atmosphere. Francesca was trembling so badly that her teeth were chattering. She tried to clench them into stillness but they just rattled inside her shocked head.

Carlo's arms folded right around her. 'It's OK,' he said then repeated it soothingly. 'It's OK…'

But it wasn't OK. His voice might be calm but the rest of him wasn't. Every muscle was clenched, pumped up and ready for whatever Angelo's anger made him do next.

What Angelo did was swing back to face them, and his

face was hard now, locked in a mould of anger and contempt. 'Let's cut to the chase,' he thrust out at Francesca. 'Looking at this little scene I interrupted, you have been behaving no better than me. So let us stop this foolishness. Come over here, Francesca,' he commanded but she noticed he didn't attempt to come and get her. 'We can talk about this later but for now we have an engagement to announce.'

He just didn't get it—or refused to get it. 'Don't you understand? It's over between us.'

'Because you think he is a better bet than me?' he sliced. 'Don't delude yourself. He doesn't want you. He's toying with you, *cara,* just for the hell of it and to get his revenge on me. Look at yourself then look at the women he usually has hanging on his arm. What do you have to compete with them?'

The cruel words flayed her already battered ego. And the contempt in his eyes flayed it some more. He might be lashing out at her in anger, but to hear and to see how much this man she'd believed loved her only an hour before actually openly disliked her was the worst blow of all.

But he was also right. A man like Carlo Carlucci had his pick where beautiful women were concerned. What could he possibly see in her?

'Don't listen,' Carlo advised in a roughened undertone. 'He wants to draw blood to salve his wounded pride.'

'He's after your money, *cara.*' Angelo fed her more poison. 'Don't kid yourself that his attention means anything more than that.'

The money. She winced. It had to come down to the wretched non-existent money. 'There isn't any money,' she sighed.

He sent her a cynically disbelieving look.

'I'm telling you the truth,' she insisted. 'I've *always* told you the truth about the money,' she added because that was just another hurt she was having to deal with—the knowledge that he'd smiled all of those careless smiles about her

Gianni connection and had been scoffing at her at the same time. 'There never has been a Gianni fortune languishing in a bank vault somewhere, waiting for me to marry before I make my claim. Whoever started that silly rumour must be rolling on the floor laughing at you by now, Angelo, because my grandfather died virtually penniless, having spent years squandering his wealth on bad investment after bad investment.' She told it more or less exactly as her great-uncle Bruno had told it to her. 'What you see at the Palazzo Gianni is basically all that's left.'

'You're lying,' he said, 'to punish me.'

'Punish you?' Her chin lifted, dusky eyebrows arching above clear hazel eyes. 'If I wanted to punish you I would be walking out of here without telling you a word of this, knowing I'd left you really festering on your loss.'

His blue eyes flicked a look at the man standing behind her. Whatever he saw in Carlo's face drained the gold out of his skin. 'You believe her,' he breathed.

'I couldn't care less if she comes dressed in rags and dragging a mountain of debts along with her so long as she does come to me,' he answered. 'And that,' Carlo added succinctly 'is the marked difference as to why you are standing where you are right now and I am standing right here...'

You had your chance and blew it, in other words. Carlo might have well said those words the way all the anger drained out of Angelo and he sank into a nearby chair then buried his face in his hands.

'What am I going to tell everyone out there?' he groaned.

Francesca could have felt a pang of sympathy for him—until he said that. Selfish to the last, he was still thinking about his own situation and wasn't showing a hint of guilt or shame for the one he'd put her in.

'Tell them the truth about your little heiress that isn't,' Carlo suggested. 'But if you can't bring yourself to do that only to be laughed at then tell them your betrothed jilted you in favour of Carlo Carlucci. At least that should win you the sympathy vote.'

Once again he was revealing his ruthlessly cutting edge. Francesca shivered as she acknowledged it. The hands at her waist tightened their grip. 'Are you ready to leave now?' He used that same edge on her next.

She hovered over giving an answer, aware that she could well be making the second biggest mistake in her life by going anywhere with him. He was ruthless to the core, easily as selfish as Angelo. And she was also aware that all that stuff about taking her in rags had been a slick cover-up to what he really believed about the Gianni fortune.

But was Carlo willing to sacrifice his freedom for it? No, the answer came back. He had too much pride in himself, too much inner strength. And he hadn't offered to marry her in Angelo's place, she reminded herself quickly. Just to get her away from here and maybe indulge in some hot sex before they parted again.

The kind of sex she'd never felt even mildly tempted to experience until she came into contact with him. That made him dangerous. She'd always known he was dangerous. Say no, she told herself. Do yourself a favour and go out there, find your friends and let them take you *safely* away from here before you drop yourself into even deeper trouble than you are already in!

'Stop thinking so much,' he rasped suddenly. 'You're no good at it right now.'

She flinched at the angry flick of his voice. He could feel her hovering indecision—feel the uncertain flutter of her heart beneath the hand he had slid up the wall of her stomach and had settled beneath the curve of her left breast. A thumb dared to move in a single light stroke against its sensitive underside and she responded with a stifled gasp.

Angelo lifted his face out of his hands, picking up the tension in the atmosphere like an animal sniffing sexual scent. 'How long have you two been two-timing me?' he demanded harshly.

It was so much like the pot calling the kettle black that she stared at him, a bubble of hysterical laughter threatening to burst in her throat.

'Not quite as long as your affair with the flatmate but long enough to know what we want.' It was Carlo who answered. He was so good at this lying business, she thought anxiously. How could she be considering putting her trust in him?

He surprised her then by lifting his hands to her shoulders, the fingers threatening to bite. She dragged her eyes away from Angelo to look into this other, darker face. He was angry, she saw. His eyes were a glitter, his mouth compressed into a grim line—not kissable, definitely not kissable right now.

'Do we leave quietly by the back way or are you up to running the gauntlet out there so you can pack your bag?'

It was both a question and a hard warning. He'd put his pride on the line here and now she was threatening to make him look a fool by wavering over going with him.

'How old are you?' she asked out of nowhere.

'Old enough to have grown out of playing games,' he said. Then he kissed her, and she learned that angry or not that mouth was indeed very kissable, hard and demanding and searingly hot—

'This is sickening.' On that muffled choke Angelo got to his feet and lurched towards the door.

'Stay where you are, *amico*,' Carlo lifted his head to toss after him. 'We still have things left to say to each other.'

Angelo froze. So did Francesca. What did they have left to say? Her skin began to prickle. She didn't like the new dark look in his eyes. 'Don't you dare discuss me with him!' she warned tautly.

'Frightened he might give your most intimate secrets away?'

She gasped, 'What's the matter with you?'

'Nothing,' he said, then on a growl of impatience lowered his mouth to her ear. 'Stop looking at him as if he's your preferred option.'

She jerked her head back to stare at him. 'But I wasn't—'

'Do we go by the back or the front?' he cut over her.

It was decision time, Francesca realised. Did she go with him or did she not? In the end it was pride that made the choice for her. What bit she had left of it was not going to let her kill it by taking the coward's way out.

So, 'The front,' she replied and wondered straight away if there was insanity in her family because, pride or not, she had to be crazy to want to go anywhere with him.

Some of the anger seeped out of him. He nodded his dark head then actually smiled. 'Brave girl,' he murmured and even kissed her for it before taking hold of her arm to lead her to the door.

He had to step around Angelo to open it for her and he did it with a smooth shift of his body that blocked the other man off from her behind the width of his wide shoulders and ignored his presence at the same time.

Ruthless, she repeated inwardly, and shivered and knew she didn't feel brave at all. The door swung open. Heaving in a deep breath, she clutched her hands into two tight fists by her sides then lifted her chin and took that first mammoth step over the threshold.

The first thing she noticed was the lack of music, then the small clutches of people dotted around the vast hall. There was a sudden drop in the hum of conversation as all faces were turned her way. What they thought they knew as fact about what was going on here and what was pure speculation was impossible to judge. That depended on which story had made the biggest impression—the one where some of them had witnessed her standing in Carlo's arms or the one where Sonya had spat out the truth about her affair with Angelo.

Her stomach muscles knotted, her throat ran sandpaper-dry. Behind her she could feel Carlo standing in the door-way as he took in their audience.

'Ten minutes long enough?' she heard him say quietly.

She swallowed and nodded, her cheeks feeling as if they would never cool down again.

'I will be here.'

It was a promise, issued loud enough for everyone to hear it. And, dangerous man or not, it was a promise she needed to hear right now.

Then she was drawing herself up, lifting her chin that bit higher and walking on legs that did not really want to support her towards the wide and sweeping marble staircase without allowing herself to make eye contact with anyone. She might not know if their expressions were vilifying her for being caught red-handed in another man's arms or if they were feeling sorry for her because she'd found out the truth about Angelo and her best friend, but one thing was certain—they would be leaning one way or the other.

It really was like walking the gauntlet. By the time she hit the stairs the low hum of conversation had begun to gather pace again. From the corner of her eye she could see Carlo's tall, dark figure still standing by the study door. No sign of Angelo. He was doing what she had been doing earlier and hiding away while he got himself together enough to face the madding crowd, or should that be buzzing crowd? she thought as she kept herself moving at a steady pace even though she wanted to run.

About halfway up, where the stairs swept around the great central chandelier, she dared to take a final peek down and saw that Angelo's parents were being ushered into the study by a grim-faced Carlo. He still didn't move from his firm stance at the door, though, watching her all the way.

Standing guard.

By the time she reached the sanctuary of her room she was almost expiring beneath the stress of it all. Closing the door behind her, she then leant back against it and closed her eyes in relief. She was trembling all over. Stupid hot tears were pricking at her eyes. She was suffering the shock and humiliation from what she had seen and overheard in the garden, she acknowledged. Was desperately confused by her own behaviour with Carlo afterwards and even more shocked by his passionately possessive behaviour towards her.

Now she was leaning here feeling frightened for the future and had the worrying suspicion that she had just committed herself to a torrid affair with the last man on earth any ordinary, sensible woman would want to become tangled up with.

Ordinary, sensible, boring, undesirable to the point where the man you intended to marry needed to supplement his passions with a real woman—a woman he'd also intended to fantasise about when he did get around to making love to her.

'Francesca…?' a wary voice murmured as if it was shooting straight out of her last bitter thought. 'Are you all right?'

She opened her eyes to see Sonya perched tensely on the end of her bed. Blue eyes big, face pale, lush mouth quivering in anxious appeal. Her heart sank like a lead weight to her stomach. 'Much you care,' she replied.

'I do care.' Sonya scrambled off the bed and began walking towards her. 'Why do you think I've been sitting here waiting for you? I needed to apologise and explain. You have to—'

'It doesn't need explaining,' Francesca cut in. 'I know what I saw, *cara*.'

The sarcastically spoken endearment earned itself a painful wince. 'I know that—don't you think I don't know that?'

Did she honestly think Francesca cared? Pushing herself away from the door, she moved at an angle that gave her the widest route around her so-called friend. Her feet took her towards the walk-in wardrobe. Sonya followed, trailing sullenly behind her.

'I need to explain to you *why* it happened,' she said pleadingly. 'You don't know the real Angelo, Francesca. He's selfish and sly. He puts on a special act for you but—'

'Not any more he doesn't.'

'No,' Sonya huskily conceded and watched as Francesca located her suitcase from where she'd stashed it just inside the room then knelt with it on the floor so she could unzip it. She had been intending to change her clothes for something more appropriate before leaving this room again but now all she wanted to do was pack her things and get out.

'You're leaving?' Sonya asked as if it was some huge surprise.

'What do you think?' It was enough to make her let loose with a strangled laugh.

She glanced up at her once closest friend to find her propping up the doorway with her arms folded defensively and looking all guilty and pale.

But she was still wearing that wretched blue satin dress, she noticed. 'You disgust me,' she said and looked away again, angry fingers unzipping the suitcase.

'I know,' Sonya surprised her by agreeing. 'I disgust myself. You know how much I hate him! I've never tried to make a secret of it but...'

They were back to the *but* Francesca didn't want to listen to. 'So how come you went out of your way to introduce this man you hate to your best friend?'

'What?' Sonya blinked her long lashes at her.

Francesca felt like slapping her face. Instead she got to her feet to go tugging clothes off hangers. 'You were living here in Rome for a whole six months before I came to join you,' she expanded, tossing clothes haphazardly down into the case. 'Your friends became my friends. You even got me my job! So how come I got no warning about the real character of this man you say you hate? How come you introduced me to him at all?'

'What was I supposed to do—ignore him when he was there with the rest?'

She had a point, Francesca conceded, though she didn't want to. She started emptying drawers. 'You wanted him for yourself even then,' she stated and only realised it was the truth as the tight words left her lips. She stopped what she was doing as full clarity began to hit. 'He wasn't interested. He already had a girlfriend. A gorgeous, dark-haired creature with amazing brown eyes…'

'Nicola,' Sonya mumbled.

Francesca nodded, and turned to look at her again. Sonya was looking at the floor now, her long hair like a heavy silk curtain hiding her face. 'You wanted to get his attention,' she went on slowly. 'So you thought you would impress him by telling him that your friend from England had some Gianni blood.'

Sonya's chin shot up. 'I didn't know he would go apoplectic at the mere mention of the Gianni name!'

'I told you that in confidence! You had no right to set that hungry wolf on to me! And once he did go apoplectic, why didn't you warn me then what you'd done?'

Sonya flushed and looked away again. Inside Francesca was beginning to seethe as each veil was scraped from her eyes. 'He took you out to pump more information out of you, didn't he? I bet he even took you to bed then!'

'As I said, I hate him.'

And she did, Francesca accepted as she stood taking in that blunt admission. Sonya hated Angelo with absolute venom but she was also so crazily in love with him she couldn't say no to him.

'He's manipulating and sly. He used me to get at you and used our friendship to stop me from telling you the truth. He said you would never forgive me—and he's right, isn't he?'

'Yes.' Francesca didn't even need to think about it. Sonya had been deeply instigative from the very beginning in setting her up for all this pain and heartache she'd had to suffer tonight because she was sure of one thing and she would not be standing here in the Batiste villa if Sonya hadn't mentioned the Gianni name.

You don't want her; you don't even like her…! Francesca sucked in a thick breath. Those cruel words were going to be etched on her soul forever now, she predicted painfully.

Bending down, she scooped up the open case with its spilling contents and pushed past Sonya to go and put the case down on the bed.

'I'm sorry,' came the husky murmur from somewhere behind her.

'You call Angelo manipulating and sly but what does that make you, Sonya?' she asked as she went about gathering up whatever other bits she'd left lying about. 'We've known each other for years. We confided everything.'

'You kept your affair with Carlo Carlucci a dark secret.' Sonya got in her own hit. 'How long has that been going on, *cara*? Don't think I missed the way you were wrapped around each other before Angelo's mother dragged me away! The room was swimming in overactive pheromones. You were both so kiss-drugged you could barely focus on anything else!'

'But at least I still had my underwear on,' Francesca retaliated with a withering slide of her eyes down the front of Sonya's dress.

She was rewarded with a choked gasp and the sight of a hand jerking down to tug guiltily at the hem of the dress. Leaving Sonya to stew on her own sluttish behaviour, she moved into the bathroom and began quickly gathering up her toiletries.

When she re-entered the bedroom she saw that Sonya was ready to go back on the attack. 'You might like to think of yourself as morally a cut above me, Francesca. But you're as guilty as I am for playing around with another woman's man.'

Was she saying that Carlo was committed to some other woman? It stopped her dead in her tracks.

'And here's the real nasty little twist, *cara*,' Sonya continued, aiming sure with her knives now. 'Nicola Mauraux—you know, the dark-haired beauty with the brown eyes you were talking about? She's Carlo Carlucci's stepsister. It was a bit of a foregone conclusion that she and Angelo would marry one day—until you came along and he turfed her out.'

Carlo was not in another relationship, was the first part of that she grabbed at with relief. Then the rest arrived like a blast, blanching the colour out of her face.

'Angelo told me it was already over,' she breathed in a stifled whisper.

'Since when has he ever spoken the truth?' Sonya asked. 'He's an incurable liar with a greedy eye for the main chance! Nicola isn't rich like you will be one day, Francesca. She isn't a Carlucci so has no claim on the Carlucci wealth. She attends this very posh university in Paris at her stepbrother's expense but that's about the sum total of what she's likely to get from him.'

'You knew all of this and didn't bother to tell me?'

'What for? I wasn't to know that you would start two-timing your beloved Angelo with Carlo Carlucci.' Oh, the knives were flying thick and fast now. This was Sonya at her cutting best. 'But if I did happen to be you right now, I would be asking if Signor Carlucci isn't using you to get back a bit of revenge on Angelo for dumping his stepsister.'

The word *revenge* hit her first. Angelo had accused Carlo of being out for revenge on him but she had been too confused to pick up on it then. He'd also said that Carlo was *using her* and she'd let that float right by her too. Then there were Carlo's displays of contempt towards Angelo and the smooth, slick, cutting way he had demolished him from the very outset—as if he'd been planning to do it—as if the whole kiss thing had been timed and rigged to happen as Angelo walked into the room!

She began to feel sick again—very sick. Her hand had to jerk up to cover her mouth. If it wasn't enough to be used by one ruthless swine, now another one had come along to do the same thing again!

Talk about being a sucker for it, she thought bitterly, and had to turn her back to Sonya so she wouldn't see the hurt tears starting in her eyes.

'I just don't want you to pile all the blame on me, that's all!' Sonya cried out. 'If you witnessed what Angelo and I were doing out there on the terrace then you must have heard me tell him that I wanted to tell you everything—and I was going to do it this time, Francesca! Only you found out before I could get to you first.'

After the sex, of course, Francesca thought bitterly. After she'd stood there on that wretched terrace and drowned herself in Angelo!

She was never going to trust a single living person, she vowed as she went to throw the last of her things into the suitcase. The tears were blurring her vision. Her fingers had developed a permanent shake. If someone had told her that she was going to spend her engagement night having her life ripped apart she would have laughed in their face!

And she still had to run the gauntlet to get out of here. She still had to face Carlo Carlucci knowing what she now knew about him!

She shut the suitcase, stuffing straggling bits of clothing inside it as she struggled to fasten the zip. Where was she going to go—what was she going to do?

'Let me come with you,' Sonya begged suddenly as if she could actually read what was going on inside her head. 'Wait for me to pack and we'll go and stay at that hotel where the rest of our group is staying.'

'Do they know about your affair with Angelo?' she asked quietly.

Silence met that—one of those stark, thick silences that screamed the answer loud and clear.

She took a final quick glance around her to see if she'd missed anything, then bent to pick up her little denim jacket and pulled it on over her dress. Next she hauled up the suitcase.

This was it. There was nothing left for her here. Mouth tight, eyes hard, she turned to walk towards the door.

'Please…' Sonya's painfully shaken cry followed her. 'Don't leave me here to face the music alone, Francesca. You're my friend—you're the only real friend I've ever had! Let me come with you—*please*!'

Francesca turned to look at this petite, flaxen-haired, sylph-like *friend* who was just too beautiful for her own good. Even the tears shining in her anxious blue eyes enhanced that beauty, as did the quiver of her lips.

'Enjoy the rest of your life, Sonya,' she said, then left with her great-uncle Bruno's chilling form of goodbye still ringing behind her like the toll of death.

CHAPTER SIX

SHE must have inherited some of the Gianni genes after all, she thought with a bitter-wry smile. Funny, she mused, but she'd always assumed she missed out on most of them. Her mother had insisted she had.

No thick and glossy raven hair, none of the Gianni bone features that had given her mother's face such a striking impact. Her mouth was too wide, her skin too pale—but that cold and unforgiving final cut she'd just used to sever her friendship with Sonya had to have come from the Gianni gene stock.

Along with her mother's propensity for falling in love with the wrong kind of man. Like lightning striking twice, or that nasty thing called fate other people liked talking about. Had it been written at her birth that she was fated to fall in love with a mercenary like Angelo then be seduced by a vengeful rat like Carlo?

She saw him then and had to pause at the top of stairs while she dealt with the way her heart dipped then shrivelled like a dried-up prune in her chest.

He was standing at the bottom of the stairs, waiting for her, looking stunning as always. The shockingly perfect profile, the smooth, olive-toned skin, the gorgeous mouth that was a mere shadowy outline from up here but could still tighten muscles all over her body on the knowledge of the way it could kiss. His black hair was making her think of ravens' wings again as it captured the overhead lights and his curling black eyelashes hovered sensuously against those chiselled cheekbones as he stood looking down at his watch.

In a rush to get this over with, *signor*? Francesca quizzed. Do you want to get the poor little fool out of here so you can finish what you started in the name of revenge?

He could have heard her for the way his dark head lifted. He smiled the most relaxed, warm smile then began walking up to meet her. 'I was just coming to get you,' he murmured in that rich, dark voice of his.

Francesca was contemplating telling him where to put his lying smile—when she noticed the people still gathered in the hall. The gauntlet, she remembered, and snapped her mouth shut again then carefully hooded her cold, glinting eyes. There was no way she was going to show herself up again while she told Carlo Carlucci what she thought of him on the Batiste staircase with the mob listening in.

The mob, she thought again, struck by her own acid turn of phrase and almost—almost found it in her to laugh. If these people were a mob they were a very exclusive kind of mob with their designer clothes and their designer jewels and their designer expressions that made her think of wax.

Carlo stopped two steps down from her and reached for her suitcase. 'Like the jacket,' he said in a husky attempt to break the tension laying whip cracks across all of them. 'It goes with the dress.'

'Can we go, please?' she responded in a voice misted with frost.

He stopped smiling, his eyes narrowing on her cold face. 'Of course,' he replied without any notable change in his rich voice tones but her senses began to scramble about inside her when they detected a change. It didn't do to return his warm overtures with ice, she realised. He was used to orchestrating the moods of others not altering his own mood to suit.

His fingers closed around her fingers where they clutched the handle to the suitcase. The suitcase changed hands within a hooded silence. Stepping to one side, he indicated that she should continue down the stairs. As she passed by him he fell into step beside her, his tall, dark bulk trying its best to hide her from most of those curious faces down in the hall.

What were they thinking? How much did they know? Was she the sinner in their eyes, caught by Angelo kissing

Carlo Carlucci on the night of his engagement to her, or the one to be pitied for falling for Angelo's smooth, slick, calculating charm at all?

Angelo—Angelo, she suddenly repeated. And felt a shaft of pain as her love for him exploded right here on this fabulous marble staircase. How could he have done this to her—treated her like this?

How could Sonya?

Delayed shock to her night of revelation really began to kick in as they made ground level. She was shaking so badly that she had a horrible suspicion she was going to further humiliate herself by falling into a sobbing huddle on the cold marble floor. Beside her, Carlo must have sensed it because his free hand came to rest against her back as if in assurance. She almost jumped out of her skin as the old warning prickles of hostility and self-defence arrived to remind her that he was not her saviour—far from it. He was as guilty as the others for trying to use her for his own ends.

'Don't touch me,' she hissed in a taut, teeth-clenched whisper.

He did the opposite. Shifting the hand until it arrived at the indent to her waist and with a single warning curl of his long fingers, he brought her into full contact with his side. Then he made the ultimate move to subdue her by stopping them walking so he could propel her around to face him, then in front of their audience he bent his dark head.

His lips arrived against her ear lobe, his breath scoring her frozen white cheek. 'Behave until we get out of here or I will kiss you stupid,' he warned very grimly.

There wasn't a split-second when she thought he might be bluffing. This was yet another man on a mission and she was just his disposable pawn. Bitterness welled, the fine tremors of dismay converting themselves into silver-shard tremors of contempt as he set them moving again.

It was then that she saw their farewell party waiting by the open front door. Mr and Mrs Batiste were standing straight-faced and soldier-like, ready to play the perfect hosts to the bitter end even as their glittering party lay in a wreck around their elegant feet. Did they know what their son had done? Had they been in on his deceit? *'Your business is safe, Papa, and don't forget who is paying the price for it.'*

Yes, they'd known from the beginning, she concluded and shuddered. Did that also mean they knew *why* she was being escorted from here by Carlo Carlucci?

Of course they did, she derided her own question. Everyone knew. Everyone knew everything but me!

'I hate you,' she hissed.

He ignored that one, the hand keeping her moving towards the open door.

'Carlo, we need to talk—' Alessandro Batiste jerked into anxious speech as they reached him.

'Next week,' Carlo Carlucci cut him off curtly, passing by him without a single pause. 'And without your son,' he added abruptly. 'If you want to hold on to my business, that is…'

'Y-yes, of course,' Angelo's father agreed in gruff obsequious Italian.

Angelina Batiste said absolutely nothing. The whole thing was a real *coup détat* for Signor Carlucci. He'd effectively cut Angelo adrift from just about everything, including the support of his own parents, it seemed.

The night air had a sharp nip to it. Carlo's car stood parked at the bottom of the steps. He guided her towards it and opened the passenger door for her and only then allowed his fingers to ease their grip on her waist when he stepped back, his expression a wall of cool politeness as he waited for her to get in the car. As she sank into luxurious black leather the door was closed with a solid click. Her eyes began to sting as she listened to him putting her case in the car boot and she had to bite down hard on her bottom lip in an effort to maintain her icy dignity as he got in beside her, folding his body like a lithe jungle cat with its killer instincts set on full alert.

It was easier to look out of the side-window than to keep him hovering even on the periphery of her vision. What she saw through that window was the door to Villa Batiste drawing shut. It was the last time she would look at that door, she vowed silently.

The car engine came to life. It kicked into gear and with a spin of wide tyres on loose gravel they moved off, the force of the acceleration pushing her back into the seat. Headlights spanned the two lines of cypress trees. They sped between them and barely paused at the junction before they were turning into the lane and accelerating away again.

She had no idea where he was taking her and at that precise moment she didn't care. Her life was in tatters. If someone had come along with a knife and cut her to ribbons she couldn't feel worse than she did right now.

Then she found that she could feel a whole lot worse when he brought the car to a sudden neck-jolting halt. She'd barely recovered from the shock of it when he was twisting towards her in his seat.

'OK,' he said. 'Tell me what your friend said to you to turn you back into the spitting cat.'

Cats and wolves were making a prominent show tonight, she thought ridiculously and almost choked on what she recognised as a lump of hysteria now blocking her throat.

'What makes you think it was Sonya?' she flashed.

'Because she was the only loose cannon out there I couldn't protect you from,' he answered.

Protect? Her eyes widened. He called this protection? She twisted her face away again, fizzing inside and refusing to answer. For a long, taut tick in time she continued to sit with her eyes still fixed on the side-window and her lips clamped tightly shut.

'Francesca!' he rasped.

'Nicola Mauraux.'

Silence. That was it. She sat there waiting for some kind of response—a guilty curse would have been enough! But nothing else happened. She wasn't breathing but he was—in and out with a calmness that set her teeth on edge. Her eyes began to sting again—she so badly wanted to break down and cry like a baby that she didn't know how much longer she could stop herself from doing it!

When he finally moved she was forced to flick another glance at him, warily unsure as to what was coming next. But all he did was settle himself back in his seat and a moment later and they were moving again as if she hadn't spoken his stepsister's wretched name.

Well—fine, she thought burningly. Let's just ignore I said it. Your silence suits me because it means I won't have to listen to you talk your slick way around the reasons why I am sitting in this car at all!

The car began to accelerate, moving very fast on the straight parts of the narrow country lane, slow and smooth through the bends with the headlights sweeping the darkness ahead of them as her grim-profiled driver put on a slick display of man versus power versus control. His timing was immaculate. He never missed a gear. The engine growled then purred then roared on acceleration then growled and purred again. And the whole thing took place beneath a heavy blanket of silence that helped to hold Francesca mesmerised even though she didn't want to be. He was the man with everything—great looks, great body and a great sense of style that utilised both to their optimum. Then there was his wealth and his power and his razor-like intellect. The way he used passion for persuasion, words like clubs to beat his opponents to death. And he drove his car with a ruthless, selfish, utter single-mindedness that dared anyone to get in his way. He reminded her of a dark, sleek, prowling predator, top of the food chain. Nothing or no one could touch him.

They sped by her great-uncle's *palazzo*. Recognising it jerked her into impulsive speech. 'You can—'

'Shut up,' he incised and made his first mistake with a gear change as if the sound of her voice was all it took to spoil his immaculate performance. The car lurched then put in a surge of power when he'd corrected the error, eating up the winding country lane with precision timing again.

And Francesca subsided in her seat as another bitter thought hit her: what was the use in demanding he take her to her uncle when the miserable old man was likely to refuse to open his door?

When disillusionment hit it stripped you of everything, she noticed, as Bruno Gianni became another name she added to her hate list. I am never going to contact him again, she vowed. He didn't care about her, hadn't even bothered to pretend that he did.

The hot ache of tears that were coming closer to bursting free by the second had her closing her eyes and huddling into her seat. As soon as this stupid journey is over I'm going home to England and I'm never going to step foot in Italy again, she promised herself. No wonder my mother never came back. No wonder she froze up whenever Italy or Rome came up in conversation. She was wise; she knew the score. *Why* hadn't she listened to her and saved herself a whole lot of grief?

They couldn't have gone more than a mile or so when the car made a sudden turn that brought her jolting back to her present situation. Her eyelids flickered upwards; she'd barely managed to focus through the tears before they were coming to another neck-jolting halt.

What now—what next? she wondered tensely.

'I w-want—'

'You don't know what you want,' he cut in tightly.

Then he was dousing the headlights and shutting down the engine with short, tight flicks of his fingers that told her he was still angry—bubbling with it. There was a click and a slither as his seat belt slid away from his body then he was opening his door and climbing into the dark night.

Her wary eyes slewed frontward, following his dark bulk as he moved around the car's long bonnet, *frissons* of uncertainty chasing across her skin. Her heart began to stutter. Was he going to eject her from his car and leave her out here in the middle of nowhere now he didn't have to bother explaining himself?

Her door came open. A waft of cold air placed a chill on her flesh. He bent down to reach across her to unlock her seat belt, and as his face arrived close to her face she saw the grim determination etched into the flat line of his mouth.

'I'm not getting out,' she informed him stubbornly.

'Does it appear that I am giving you a choice?' he asked. Then grabbed one of her hands as he straightened up again, and used it to haul her out of the car.

She arrived beside him in a state of numbing panic, sights and sounds hitting her senses at the same time as his body did. His arm came round her waist, arching her into full contact with his lean, hard length at the same time that she heard the car door shut behind her and another sound of whirring that had her twisting her head in time to see a pair of huge, thick wrought-iron gates swinging shut beneath a heavy stone arch she hadn't even been aware that they'd passed beneath.

Dizzy and disorientated, she became aware of uneven cobblestones beneath her thin-soled shoes and turned her head again in an effort to search the darkness for some hint as to where they were. Her mouth brushed his chin as she moved and his hissed sound of his tense response brought her search to a stop on his face. Then she wasn't seeing anything but the angry flame of desire leaping in his dark eyes, the savage tautening of his skin and flaring nostrils as he took in a swift breath of air. She felt a sudden tightening in his body, sucked in her own shocked gasp when she realised what the tightening meant. Her gaze dipped lower—

to his mouth...his hard, tight, angry mouth that was already advertising what was going to come next.

'No—' She managed that one breathlessly weak protest before he made full contact. After that she wasn't capable of saying or doing a single thing as his mouth moulded hers and his tongue made its first stabbing thrust. She was instantly electrified, fierce heat pouring a hot, tight sting of pleasure right down her front to gather in a sense-energising pool at her thighs.

She groaned and clutched at his shoulders, so shocked by her own response that she tried to push away from him, but it was a wasted effort because he only had to use the flat of his hand against the arching base of her spine to bring her in contact with his hard, muscular front for her to go weak at the knees.

He felt them go, felt her whole body quiver as a helpless little moan of pleasure keened in her throat. If this kiss was meant to be a punishment then it had failed in its mission, she found herself thinking dizzily as she went willingly when he pulled her even tighter up against him and she was kissing him back as she'd never kissed anyone, with a wild, deep, urgent hunger that took her over completely.

A powerful light suddenly drenched the two of them. The kiss broke abruptly, and on a curse Carlo twisted with her still wrapped against him while Francesca buried her face in his dinner jacket and quite simply lost the will to live. Her senses had shattered. She'd thought they'd done that earlier tonight when she'd watched Angelo with Sonya. But even that devastating moment could not compare with how she was dealing with the loss of that unbelievable kiss.

'My apologies, *signor*,' a deeply contrite male voice murmured in Italian from somewhere close by. 'The security lights are not functioning. I had to come myself to see—'

'Take that damn torch off my face, Lorenzo,' Carlo commanded in a harsh, rasping growl.

They were thrown into instant darkness again. Francesca managed to unclip her fingers from where they clung to Carlo's neck. From feeling virtually incandescent with pleasure she was now slowly sinking into horror and shame.

She hated him! How could she have responded like that to a man she absolutely hated?

She tried to stiffen away from him but he was having none of it, his grip only tightening warningly as he held some kind of intelligent discussion with what she presumed was a security guard though she couldn't be sure of anything right now. Her feet felt strange, as if they didn't belong to her, her legs were tingling from ankles to hips. And the dragging sensation taking place between her thighs was desperate enough to tug a thick whimper from her aching throat.

Whatever Carlo thought that whimper meant, he reacted to it with another black curse and suddenly she was being thrust beneath the power of one arm and forced to walk.

'Let me go,' she choked out. Being this close to him was beginning to take on the properties of a nightmare—the whole evening was!

'Not in the near future, *cara*,' he responded with dry, grim sarcasm that was so thick with sexual reference that she stumbled.

He kept her upright. He kept her moving over uneven cobblestones. He kept her wrapped so closely to him that she had difficulty trying to take in her surroundings though she did manage to note that they were walking across an enclosed courtyard that made her footsteps echo off the surrounding walls. She could also hear the soft sound of a fountain somewhere, saw dark blue paintwork framing long, narrow windows set into burnt-sienna-painted walls.

Then they were stopping in front of a door. Muscles flexed as he leant forward to grasp the handle, the grasp of his long fingers sliding upwards a small inch that was all it required to let her right breast know they were there. She sucked in a sharp gasp as a fresh wave of heat poured in that direction. If it hadn't been for the denim jacket helping to conceal what was happening to her she would have folded with embarrassment when she felt the nipple grow excruciatingly tight.

The door swung open with a twist of the handle, and she was being propelled through it into a fully lit long, wide hallway with faded blue walls and gold-leaf plasterwork. He didn't so much as pause as he began hustling her over a stunning blue mosaic floor towards the other end of the hall. They passed by a pair of staircases that sped off at right angles, one on either side of them, passed beautiful pieces of furniture that were in themselves priceless works of art. Everything she set her dizzy eyes on was stunningly tasteful and elegant, nothing bore so much as a vague resemblance to the Batistes' white villa with its overt grandeur and style.

Another door was flung open and once again she was being ushered firmly through it into a square-shaped room with more gold-leaf plasterwork, chalk-pale terracotta walls and yet another mosaic floor made up of brown and black marble inlaid with gold.

At last he let her go and she swayed a little as she looked for balance, then instantly spun round as the door was slotted into its frame. Eyes wide, control shot, unsure whether she should be terrified or just plain angry after that shocking kiss and the way he'd hustled her in here, 'W-what is this place?' she demanded. 'Why have you brought me here?'

His smile had a sinister cut to it. The way he folded his arms across his impressive chest, crossed his elegant black shoes at his ankles then leant those broad shoulders back against the door and even the glitter behind his narrowed eyes were displays of arrogant provocation that brought every nerve-end she had left ringing on full alert.

'Welcome, to the Palazzo del Carlucci,' he murmured smoothly. 'Home to my family for the last four centuries and now, *mi amore*, the venue for your complete ravishment—in the honourable name of *revenge*, of course.'

As a calculated heart-stopper he had certainly hit the perfect note, Carlo saw as he watched all colour drain from her face. His sarcastic tone had slid right by her and he was angry enough not to care.

No, he was more than angry—he was bloody furious! He'd put his reputation on the line for her tonight. He'd watched over her, been there to catch her when she'd fallen, found her time and the privacy to come to terms with the reality of what Batiste was really like. He'd protected, supported—smiled in the face of a hundred scandalised stares while he got her out of that situation as fast as he could. And what did she do?

She took the word of a lying tramp like her flatmate and turned him into the enemy!

'Lay a hand on me and I'll claw your eyes out,' she responded shakily to his silk-honed threat.

He sent her a smile that mocked and derided. 'Since we both know that my laying *both* hands on you is more likely to make you purr than claw, it was a rather wasted threat, don't you think?'

It was like feeding candy to a baby, he noted. She grabbed every word and swallowed it whole. In some dark corner of his anger he enjoyed watching her squirm in growing alarm. He even shifted his stance as if to come after her, just to see how she would react.

She took a step back. 'Stay right where you are!' she jerked out sharply and put out a hand to ward him off.

Some chance, he thought. The ravishment was becoming more appetising by the second. And that kiss-softened quivering mouth was just begging to be ravished again—and again. If her beautiful eyes went any darker they would be the same colour as his own eyes, which made him very curious as to how dark they were going to go in the throes of some very intense passion.

'I will be no one else's victim—especially not yours!'

'Why not mine? When you don't think twice about playing the willing victim for anyone who wants to beat you up with their lies?'

'Whose lies are you referring to?' She threw a puzzled frown at him. It hit him low in his loins like a kick. He'd never known a simple dusky frown could be so damn sexy, it sent his shoulders shifting tensely inside his dinner jacket.

'Are you saying that Nicola Mauraux *isn't* your stepsister?'

'No,' he sighed. 'I am not saying that.'

'Then what are you saying? Do you think tonight has been a ball of laughter for me, *signor*? Do you think I *want* to be standing here listening to you play stupid word-games just for the fun of it?'

He went to answer but wasn't given the chance to. 'I am not the one at fault for whatever Angelo did to your stepsister,' she told him in trembling self-defence. 'As far as I knew they'd finished their relationship when Nicola returned to her studies in Paris!' she cried. 'I do not steal other women's men from them. And I will not take the blame because your stepsister was hurt! If you want your revenge look to Angelo—and show a little class by moving away from that door so that I can leave!'

Well, well, Carlo thought curiously, narrowing his eyes on her stiff if trembling stance, and had to acknowledge that his tables had just been turned. It came as a surprise because he hadn't thought she had it in her to take him on with quite so much ego-shredding venom.

Show a little class, he repeated musingly to himself, and almost smiled at the hit that cutting remark had landed on his pride.

'And here I was, waiting for you to apologise to me for daring to believe the word of some vamped-up little tramp in really deep trouble, who thought she would stick a few knives in by telling you that I was capable of using you for the purposes of revenge!'

His voice had risen in anger; now she was staring at him through huge shocked eyes. 'I...' she began.

'From there I thought we would continue where we left off in the courtyard,' he continued ruthlessly without letting her speak. 'With some really deep, passionate sex—preferably in my very big, comfortable bed, where we would work to help clear away your quite understandable blues.'

Her chin shot up at the very deliberate way he had just casually dismissed the devastation she had to be suffering.

'*After* the sex we could then discuss Nicola and how the whole Carlucci clan is in your debt for luring Batiste into believing that the Gianni fortune would be more accessible than hers would be.'

At last she was beginning to realise that this conversation had another edge to it. He could see a slow dawning colouring her eyes.

'However,' he went on, 'if you prefer to leave then by all means do so.' He even straightened from the door to give her safe passage. 'There is a phone in the hall and a pad lying next to it with the number of a very good taxi service. If I were you I would get the driver to recommend a hotel for the night and avoid going back to your apartment—just in case you walk in on your best friend and your ex-fiancé indulging their lusts on the sitting-room carpet.'

Having watched her blanch at his final cut-throat comment, he strode across the room, arrogantly assured that he had recovered his ego—at the expense of hers.

Did that knowledge sit well on him? No, it didn't, he admitted with a grimace. But one of them had to climb off their high horse and, since he had no intention of doing it, it had to be Francesca.

He was a full-blooded Carlucci after all. She was only half a Gianni.

And anyway, he was still angry despite his smooth, careless speech. There were a million things he could have been doing out there if he hadn't been devoting his full and undivided attention to Francesca Bernard and her Cinderella plight!

Cinderella, he scathed as he approached the antique French armoire almost dominating one wall. Well, if that made him her Prince Charming then he wasn't doing a very good job of it, he conceded as he glared at the armoire his stepmother had brought with her from Paris when she married his father.

As he opened the doors he smelled the age of the solid old wood. Inside had been converted into a comprehensive drinks cabinet, which had always seemed a desecration to him but—he offered another grimace. Nanette had been proud of it and in the end that was all that mattered. This single piece of furniture had been her one and only heirloom and she'd loved to see it sitting here in this great house that groaned beneath centuries of Carlucci statements to wealth and good taste. What else she brought into this house had always been far more valuable.

It was called love and happiness. And for those gifts alone the armoire would remain exactly where it stood for as long as he held power of decision over the house.

Reaching for the bottle of cognac and a deep-bowled glass, he was aware that Francesca still hadn't made that move towards the door. Placing the bowl of the glass in his palm to warm it while he uncapped the bottle of cognac, he dared a sideways glance at her.

She looked like a pale and bewildered ghost, he observed. Her eyes were too wide and rimmed by the stinging threat of tears that placed a fine quiver on her mouth. She was trying to control it, trying her best to maintain some pride and dignity. But she wasn't standing where he was standing and seeing what he was seeing. She looked vulnerable, exhausted, so damn shattered he was amazed she was still in one piece.

Her skin looked so strained it was waxen. And her hair was trying its best to escape again, the beaded comb barely clinging to the twisted silken knot.

But not for long, he promised himself as he turned away again. He was going to help the hair out in a minute. He was going to remove the silly comb and let the whole tawny mass tumble free. And he was going to heat that waxen flesh until it melted. He was going to remove that silly denim jacket then that silly dress with its romantic layers of chiffon that did nothing for her and yelled 'bought to please Angelo Batiste!'.

Anger growled like a snarling dog inside him; his lips bit together to stop the sound from coming out.

He was going to strip her down to her wonderful skin and bin the whole bloody outfit. Then he was going to begin the task of rebuilding her from the inside out. He was going to turn her into what he perceived she would be if she hadn't had her self-confidence beaten to a pulp by inadequate selfish swines like Bruno Gianni and Batiste.

But for now he was going to have to continue to play it tough here, because she also looked like a trapped bird trying to sum up the courage to make a bolt for escape. If she did then he was going to have to stop her—and cornered, trapped birds had a nasty habit of flying at your face.

He poured a generous splash of cognac into the glass then swirled it around while deftly recapping the bottle with his free hand. By the time he turned back to her he was relieved to find that she'd moved at last and was no longer staring vacantly into space but was looking up at the gilt-framed portrait hanging above the huge stone fireplace, in which his father stood with his arms linked around the slender frame of the beautiful dark-haired Nanette. Nanette was looking up, his father was gazing down, and only a blind idiot would miss the wealth of love and affection that poured from every brushstroke.

'You look like him,' she said.

'Mm,' he acknowledged with a small wry smile. 'Nanette Mauraux was my father's second wife,' he explained as he walked towards her. 'My mother died when I was—quite young.'

He offered her the glass. Francesca shook her head, her attention still fixed on the portrait. 'That could be Nicola standing with him,' she said.

'Does Nanette look so young?' Turning to view the portrait for himself, 'Yes, she does,' he answered his own question. 'My father managed to shock all of Rome when he went to Paris on a business trip and came back with a child bride clinging to his arm...'

He took a sip of the brandy, remembering. Then offered a soft laugh. 'He was fifty-four and she was twenty-three. Nicola was a tiny replica of her *mama* and I was a brooding, dark, resentful youth of nineteen who was appalled to be presented with a stepmother I would probably have made a play for if I'd met her first.'

'Did you?' she looked at him. 'Make a play for her, I mean.'

It took him a few seconds to understand why she dared think such a thing of him. Then, 'Ah,' he smiled. 'I forgot—I have no scruples.'

It was the wrong thing to say. He knew it the moment the comment left his sardonic mouth. She stared at him for a second—then on a small choke she turned and ran.

On a thick black curse he went after her, having to pause to divert to the armoire to lose the brandy glass before continuing on. She'd already thrown the door open and was disappearing into the hall. He uttered another terse curse in Italian. His trapped bird had flown but in her eagerness to get away from him she'd turned the wrong way.

CHAPTER SEVEN

FRANCESCA knew what she'd done two flying steps along the hallway but there was no way she was turning around and risking passing that door just as he came out of it.

She'd had enough. She just couldn't take any more of his cruel sarcasm and anyway, she'd already spied a pair of doors standing shut ahead of her so she just kept going, not caring where those doors led to as long as she managed to put a distance between herself and the hateful Carlo Carlucci before she finally gave in and fell apart.

What she didn't expect was to drag open those two doors and take two more flying steps, only to come to a perfect standstill, held breathless, feeling as if she'd stepped out of that door and straight into a completely different world.

Lake Alba was floating right in front of her, its smooth surface wearing a moonlit glaze like a sheet of frosted white silk. She had never seen anything quite like it. She forgot she was supposed to be running away from Carlo's taunting as she stared through a stone archway supported by twin slender pillars that framed the lake like a painting, its base trimmed by a low stone latticework balustrade that seemed to form an edge to the end of the world.

It was the most magical scene she had ever encountered; nothing had prepared her for it on the swift journey here through the winding lanes. Villa Batiste claimed a view of the lake but nothing to compare with this one. They were so close—yet not very close at all. It was a strange very disorientating sensation to stand here and feel as if you could reach out and touch those silver silk waters yet be aware at the same time that acres of layered garden lay in between.

Her feet took her across the wide stone terrace, drawing her like a magnet to stand beneath the arch. She was so enchanted she didn't notice that she was shivering so badly that her arms had wrapped around her in an instinctive attempt to ward off the cold.

'The lake changes with every hour,' a deep voice murmured levelly. 'She will pull on her shimmering silver cloak in the early morning, a burnished gold one in the late afternoon. In the middle of the day she wears a sensational azure-blue cloak and invites you to come and play…'

'So you framed it,' she said softly.

'One of my ancestors was inspired by that particular vision,' he replied in a lazy tone that reluctantly refused to take the praise. Then she heard the slow, even pace of his steps bringing him closer as he continued, 'We are in fact standing in a colonnade of arches, each one carefully placed to form the same framework of the lake whichever door or window you happen to step through in this wing.'

A fleeting glance sideways confirmed that she was indeed standing in the middle of a line of arches that attached to the house by long, gracefully arching ribs on which the moonlight placed more frosted silk.

'It's beautiful—the whole thing.' She turned her head frontward again as he came to a halt directly behind her.

'Gratzi,' he replied at the same time as his jacket settled across her shoulders and was held there by a pair of hands that curled around her slender upper arms. She shivered compulsively as her chilled flesh grabbed at the warmth the jacket offered. 'No, cara, don't prickle.' He'd misread the shiver. 'I am not about to renew hostilities.'

Then what does come next—the ravishment? she heard herself thinking. And this time the shiver was a prickle.

'I'm sorry if I hurt your stepsister,' she felt compelled to say.

'You didn't—he did.' His grip on her arms altered fractionally so he could turn her round to face him. She found herself staring at the bright white front to his shirt. 'All I could do was support her through her heartache. While I was doing that I became curious as to who this new woman in his life was, who could make him dare to hurt one of mine.'

'So whose wounded pride were you out to salve when you went looking for a way to punish him—your stepsister's or your own?'

This time it was the cleft in his chin that captured her attention when it flexed with his brief, dry smile. 'Try— both,' he said and moved his fingers, causing her breathing to feather as he ran them lightly beneath the silk lapel to his jacket, lifting the fabric so it hugged her chilly nape. 'And you have a novel way of making subtle stabs at a man's ego, *cara*,' he said softly. 'But I advise you to drop such tactics with me. You see, I *like* my arrogance. It gives me leave to do anything I want to do even when I know the moment is not appropriate.'

And that was the point when alarm bells began to ring. She managed only to lift wary eyes to his face and note the warning gleam of what was to come before he gave a firm tug on his jacket collar and she was arriving with a breathless gasp against his chest. She felt the heat of him, his sheer physical power, wanted to push away but only found herself raising her chin.

Their eyes connected, almost black consuming anxious hazel with promises that robbed her of the ability to breathe.

'No,' she said, 'don't…'

And to her hopeless confusion he didn't do anything but hold her trapped between his body and his jacket and a tense, tingling limbo world between heaven and hell. She couldn't even tell which the hell belonged to—the kiss or no kiss.

'Sure?' he said softly.

She nodded, lips parted and trembling like wicked liars. He was too much—of everything. He overwhelmed in every way there was. 'I'm out of my depth with you,' she heard herself whisper and though she wished the words back the moment she'd said them she knew they were telling the utter truth.

His response was one of those sardonic tilts to his mouth. 'I am wading in pretty deep myself, *cara*,' he responded huskily. 'So don't let yourself think that those pale cheeks and that frightened expression is going to save you. We *will* come together sooner or later.'

Then he dropped his head, capturing her lips in a single swift, hard kiss that fused them together with its heat. 'Again and again and again…' he murmured with sensual promise as he lifted his mouth away.

Why? Because she'd responded. He knew it. She knew it. She'd even been the one to taste him with the moist, tingling tip of her tongue and placed that gloss on his lips she could see. And the worst of it was she wanted to do it again. She wanted to curl a hand around his nape and bring that mouth back to her. She wanted to…

His chest heaved on a tense intake of air, dark eyes glittering now as he took in the helpless expression colouring her eyes. 'Come on,' he said with a low gruffness. 'It's too damn cold out here for this…'

This being that she had just committed herself. *This* being that she couldn't even pretend to herself that she didn't want him. Letting go of his jacket lapels, Carlo placed an arm round her shoulders and turned them back to the house.

The door closed behind them; centuries-old blue mosaic caught the tap of her delicate heels. She wanted to say something—anything to break the grim, sexual resolve she could feel pulsing in him. But there wasn't a single word that came to mind that could halt what was now in flow.

He led her up the left-hand staircase, his arm still keeping her close to his side. They emerged from the stairs into another long corridor flanked by long, narrow windows she saw looked out on the courtyard below. He paused at a door, pushed it open and took her through it. She found herself standing in a bedroom like no other bedroom she had ever been in.

The floor was an ocean of polished dark wood that led her eyes to the huge stone fireplace opposite where logs blazed in a black iron grate. The flames flickered across the floor, the dark terracotta-painted walls and crawled like fingers up the swathes of dark red silk festooning a huge canopied four-poster bed.

The bed dominated the room above everything. It dominated her—grabbed her eyes and fixed the senses exactly where it intended to fix them. If she'd ever wondered what a room designed to pull all the right sensual strings looked like then this would have been it. She even captured an image of herself lying there naked like a wanton on the red silk coverlet. She saw him with his dark golden flesh touched by the flames as he lay at her side.

The vision alone was enough to put her right back into a panic. She turned on him. 'I don't…'

Want this, she had been going to say but the words became lost in the feel of his light touch as he plucked the comb from her hair. The heavy twist quivered as it uncoiled its way to her shoulders. He stood observing the effect through dark, unfathomable eyes for a long moment then abruptly turned away.

'I'll go and get your case,' he said. 'Relax, take a look around, I won't be more than a few minutes…'

Threat or reassurance? Francesca wondered as she watched him disappear. Then she shivered and turned back to her new surroundings. Her gaze was instantly drawn to the four-poster bed, where those unnerving images still played with her head.

Shame on you, she tried telling herself and tugged her eyes away then moved restlessly across the room towards a long window draped with more red silk. The window showed her a different view of the lake. Its surface wasn't quite as frosted now, the moon having already continued on its way.

What am I doing here? she asked herself.

An answering tug on certain sensitive folds of flesh made her draw in air on a sharp catch of breath.

'Oh,' she choked, and dropped down onto the polished wood window seat, lost her shoes then pulled her knees up to her chin and dragged Carlo's jacket tightly around her before she lowered her face to her knees.

To hide.

From what she was.

From what she was beginning to turn into.

A betrayed woman with the terrible—terrible desire for another man.

She shuddered, despising herself for feeling like this. Still hurting in so many ways and clearly so darn desperate to prove she was worthy of the title "woman" that she was sitting here having to squeeze her thighs together in an attempt to cut off these tight little tugs that were so much a pleasure as well as a sin.

Sin.

She picked out the word and looked at it. What sin? Whose sin? Where was the sin in wanting to make love?

Her mother's sin. Her mother's cold assessment of what sexual desire could do to you. It could turn you into a slave to your own body cravings and the faceless property of the man who took those cravings and used them to slake his own.

Why him though? If she had to turn into this sex-needy person, why did it have to be for Carlo Carlucci of all men? Why couldn't it have been Angelo? Maybe their relationship could have stood a better chance if she'd been more forthcoming on the physical side. Maybe he would not have gone looking elsewhere and the rest of this dreadful night would only exist in some far-off nightmare and she would be in bed by now—with Angelo—sublimely content in her blindness to what his true character really was like.

Is that what she wanted? she then asked herself. To be lied to so long as she didn't have to face the miserable truth?

She heard his step in the half-open doorway, felt him pause when he saw the way she was sitting here. Tears burned. Her heart burned. That place between her thighs grew hot on a fresh flurry of excitement because she wanted him.

She wanted him.

Not Angelo. She had never wanted Angelo. Not like this, she groaned silently. Blind didn't begin to excuse the way she had been behaving around Angelo in the name of that thing called love.

'I've brought your case.'

She nodded. Love was nothing but an illusion anyway, she thought as she listened to his footsteps taking him across to the bed. Love was nothing but a word invented for women to use to justify giving in to this hot sexual ache and for men to use to give them the right to tap into that ache.

Her head twisted at the sound of his footsteps. Heat gathered in her cheeks this time, her eyes glued to him as she followed his approach. Tall, dark, breathtakingly alluring to her newly awoken senses, they drank in the width of broad shoulders and long, lean torso covered in white shirting that did nothing to hide the promise of what she envisioned lurked beneath. The butterfly collar of the shirt had been unfastened and the bow-tie now rested in two loose black strips against the shirt.

He looked relaxed; he even offered her one of his tilted smiles as he bent to take hold of her hands to break the clasp they held on her knees.

'Come on,' he said quietly. 'You've had enough. It's time to go to bed.'

He pulled and she uncoiled to land on her feet in front

of him. Removing the jacket from her shoulders, he tossed it onto the window seat then turned his attention to the line of bronze studs holding her denim jacket in place.

The word bed made her throw a hooded glance at him, the way he was casually removing her clothes tingled her spine—and he smiled again at those two very revealing actions. 'It's OK. The ravishment of Francesca Bernard has been put on hold for the time being,' he assured her lazily.

'Shame,' she heard herself say—then caught her top lip between her teeth and wished the floor would open up and swallow her when he went perfectly still. She attempted a weak smile. 'Joke,' she said.

He went back to what he'd been doing but his mouth had a grim look of disapproval about it now.

Disapproval? she repeated inwardly and uttered a thick laugh. The person who disapproved of her around here was herself!

'Why the laugh?'

'Don't ask,' she advised a little wildly. Because the cool backs of his fingers were brushing against her breasts and making them tingle and if anyone wanted the ravishment of Francesca Bernard then it was Francesca Bernard!

Denim parted and was eased from her shoulders. She shivered as the fabric trailed down her arms, exposing her flesh to the cooler air seeping in through the window behind. The jacket landed on the window seat on top of his jacket then, with the touch of a master at undressing women, he slid his hand to the side of her ribcage to locate unerringly the concealed zip that held the dress in place.

'I can do the rest myself,' she told him stiffly.

'Why rob me of the pleasure?' he mocked—silkily—bringing her eyes up to clash with his.

He knew what she was thinking, what was happening to her, what she *wanted* to happen. And the look in his eyes was daring her to just come out and say it.

Ask! that look challenged.

She looked away again—moved away. His hand pulled her back again. She came into full contact with his full length. Her senses took flight on a mad ride of desire, she shivered and shook and sparked up like a firework. Her breathing fractured, her breasts heaved a gasp. His free hand lifted to burrow beneath her hair and his fingers clenched, imprisoning a thick swathe of her hair to use it to pull her head back.

She couldn't tell if his eyes were angry or on fire with desire. His mouth still looked hard, his cheekbones taut. 'What do you want from me, Francesca?' he demanded on a low, dark growl.

The impact of the question quivered its way right down to her toes because she knew exactly what she wanted from him. She wanted him to give her sensual escape. She wanted to lose herself in him and become that other person she had just seen lying in naked abandon on that bed.

And she wanted to emerge the other end of this dreadful night a completely different woman, a sexually liberated woman who could state with confidence—to hell with you, Angelo, I know what I am now and you will never know what you missed out on!

'I want everything,' she whispered.

There, she'd said it. She didn't even regret saying it, she told herself defiantly as his eyes narrowed on her flushed face. Now it was up to him whether he took what she was offering or rejected it.

He didn't reject it. He took with a swift, dark passion that blew her apart. Her mouth was taken, its inner recesses invaded by the urgent probe of his tongue. She joined in this electric-charged fire dance with an eagerness that could have suggested she always kissed like this, when the opposite was the truth. It didn't matter, she was with that kiss all the way—totally committed to it, totally committed to greedily learning anything he could teach her that would fuel the fires of what was happening to her. The side zip to her dress gave suddenly, the tight bodice springing free so the dress fell without stopping to the floor, leaving him free to explore new areas of exposed flesh with one hand while the other maintained its fierce grip on her hair to keep her face turned up to the kiss.

It was a very potent display of masculine domination— she knew that even as she surrendered to it. He stroked her waist, her back, her shoulders, he ran his fingers beneath the thin back strap to her flimsy strapless bra—testing its tension before trailing those fingers down the indent of her spine to the edge of her very brief high-leg panties to test their tension as his hand slid beneath.

She'd never felt a man's hand against the smooth, rounded flesh of her bottom before. She'd never been touched like this at all. It felt strange but so exquisitely sensual she wriggled. He gripped and lifted her into contact with what was happening to him.

The movement tangled her feet in silk organza. On a curse he released her mouth so he could glance down. She was panting and clinging to his neck, too delirious to notice the way his eyes paused to linger blackly on the rise and fall of her breasts cupped in blood-red silk that was losing the battle to keep the tight thrust of her nipples covered. On a soft growl he clamped an arm around her waist and lifted her off the floor to swing her free of the dress—then he held her there, trapped against him, and closed his mouth around one of her breasts. The hot lick of his tongue sliced an arcing sense of tight pleasure across the tight nipple. She gasped out a thick breath, shaken and shuddering, her fingers clutching at his shoulders, and he tugged on her hair again to arch her backwards to bring the other breast pointing invitingly upwards for the delivery of the same experience.

Then they were kissing again, and he was turning with her still clamped against him as he walked towards the bed. That was not all he did on that short journey. With the strength of his hands he lifted her higher, somehow guiding her legs around his hips. The pulsing centre of all this madness made contact with the bulging hardness of his penis and her hips lurched in shock then writhed as a new pulsing wave of pleasure caught fire.

As he let her slide slowly down his length her bra sprang free. Two full, rounded breasts fell out of their bra cups, and she looked down to watch with a kind of fascination as their stinging tips settled against his shirt front.

He muttered something. She looked up into blazing black eyes and an oddly pale complexion. 'Are you sure you want this?'

She gave him his answer by capturing his mouth with a reckless hunger. When he broke away from her she felt bereft.

Then not so bereft when he began stripping his clothes off, watching her as she stood watching him with a strange mix of fascination and shyness flickering across her expressive face. His shirt was peeled off and tossed away to reveal broad shoulders that gleamed like satin in the fire glow, and a taut, bronzed torso matted with dark hair. His shoes were heeled off and kicked to one side then his fingers went to deal with the fastener and zip to his trousers—and that was the moment when she had to look away.

Her eyes went straight to the bed with its red silk coverlet and its flame-licking promise of what was to come. She dragged in a breath, her senses fluttering on the beginnings of uncertainty, but that was all the time she was given to doubt this because his hand snaked out to cup her chin and he was making her look back at him. He was naked—naked, and so utterly beautiful it was no wonder he could strip with such ease.

His mouth closed over hers again, not fierce but gentle and soft. His other arm coiled around her waist and slowly drew her in. Nothing had prepared her for what it felt like to be held against a naked man. The warmth of him, the intoxicating differences between smooth and rough textures, the heady power of his scent, the unyielding strength in him, the uncompromising evidence of his manhood pressing against her abdomen and the way he moved against her leaving her in no doubt as to how much he wanted this. She released a shaken little breath in response to that knowledge and he stole it from her with a flick from his tongue.

He kissed the heat burning in her cheeks, her shyly lowered eyelids—he drew her that bit closer to him then pressed moist kisses to her shoulder, her neck, then her mouth again while she stood absorbing each tiny pleasure without being aware of how still she was.

'If you've changed your mind and want to stop, this is the moment to say so,' he said gently.

She frowned, not understanding why he kept asking that question. 'I don't want to stop.'

'Then why are your hands clenched into fists at your sides?'

They were…?

They were, she realised as she tried to move her fingers, only to find they'd locked in two tension fists.

'I will not make love to a sacrifice, *cara*. If you're standing here like this, hoping to God I will wipe Batiste's loving into oblivion, then you are wasting your time because neither do I play substitute for another man.'

The fact that she'd believed he'd understood, from what he'd overheard Angelo say to Sonya, that she had never been with Angelo like this made her frown as she stared fixedly at the crisp dark coils of hair on his chest. Now she knew he must have misunderstood, there was no way she was going to expose just how little Angelo had wanted her, by telling him the truth.

'I w-wasn't thinking anything of the kind,' seemed a fair compromise.

'Then why the tension?'

Her lips quivered; she tugged in a breath. 'Y-you,' she

told him shakily. 'You're so...' She ran the nervous tip of her tongue around her lips.

If she'd conjured up the excuse just to flatter him she could not have found a better one. He laughed, low and throatily, then moved against her in a way that left her in no doubt as to how her little confession was affecting him.

Then he wasn't laughing, he was dipping his dark head, and suddenly the whole thing became intense again. The deep, drugging kisses, the caressing sweep of his hands. The gentle, pulsing movement of his hips that slowly—slowly began to draw answering movements from her. When he hooked an arm around her waist and used it so he could feed her onto the bed he did it with such smooth control that she wasn't even aware of what was happening until she felt cool cotton beneath her and opened her eyes to stare in surprise.

The red coverlet had been tossed aside without her noticing, the rest of the covers folded back. And Carlo's lean, dark golden length was caught by the fire again as he stretched out beside her, then came to lean above her, his dark eyes languid now, sensually engrossed as he sent a hand stroking the length of her body, then began touching light, soft, tantalising kisses in a delicate line along her mouth then across her cheek to her temple and down along her jaw line before returning to her mouth again. Her tongue made its first shy stab between his teeth, her fingers curling into his hair in an effort to hold him still. He let her keep him, he let her trace the moist inner recesses of his mouth and play with the kiss as she'd never played before.

His hand came to cup her breast, the pad of his thumb gently circling the dusky aureole in a slow, breathtaking caress. His mouth moved on again, planting soft kisses along her throat and across the pale slopes of her breast before it closed a tight pink rosebud nipple inside a warm, moist, gently sucking mouth. Sensation became a low deep throbbing ache that spread its sensual fingers to every part of her, quickening her pulses and dragging on her breath. He gave the other breast the same slow, sensual pleasure, his hand gently kneading in tune with his lips until she groaned in sweet agony to it all.

As if the little sound was a sign that stirred his blood his mouth suddenly was back on hers again, taking with driving, hungry passion at the same time his hand trailed a caressing passage down her ribcage to the flat of her stomach before moving on, smooth fingertips slipping beneath the flimsy triangle of raspberry silk and spearing through the dusky mound of curls on a seeking quest.

Shock turned her limbs to liquid, her shaken choke broke their kiss. She opened her eyes and found herself staring directly into naked desire burning molten in the fire glow as his fingers discovered the heart of her. Alien though it was, she squirmed on a wave of white-hot pleasure, her heart pounding at a thundering pace, her fingers clawing at his shoulders as he dipped, withdrew, caressed then dipped again with the smooth, sure touch of a man who knew exactly how to make a woman feel like this. Wild, she felt wild, caught in a slipstream of scintillating pleasure that flowed through her blood. She arched against him, quivering, her breathing reduced to tight, aching little gasps. He captured one of her breasts and she leapt, she shuddered, she sank beneath the rolling surface of shattering sensation and fought him like a mad woman but clung to him desperately at the same time.

And he was hot, his breathing thick and tense, each lithe movement of his body such a sensual act she didn't know which part of him was going to inflame her next. He murmured something in Italian but she was way beyond being able to translate. The sensual, soothing sound of his voice impinged, though; the gentle brush of his hand across her cheek.

She opened her eyes to find he was frowning—at her naive lack of control no doubt. 'I'm not…' used to this, she was about to confess, but he hushed her into silence with the warm crush of his mouth.

Then she was losing herself again in a world made up of pure feeling. He trailed kisses across her breasts, catching each distended nipple and rolling it with his tongue. He kissed her all over. He explored her like a master and she responded with a writhing and whimpering then groaning in protest when his trailing mouth moved to the singing sensitivity of her groin. He kissed her hip, her waist and finally her breasts again, then recaptured her mouth at the same time as he reached for one of her hands and gently curled it around his sex.

It was a shock, a mind-rocking shock to feel the smooth, thick length of a man's sexual power then experience its surge of pleasure to her touch. As he moved she found herself curling towards him with an instinctive need to be closer than close. Her mouth found his throat and fastened there, her breasts pressed against his chest. Her untutored hand clasped him as he moved with small, slow, delicate thrusts. She could feel his heart pounding and the tautness grow in his body as the sensual fever grew. And through it all his fingers sustained their gentle, knowing caresses with an expertise that sank her deeper and deeper into a place she had never been before.

'Carlo...' she said on a breathless whimper but didn't know why she needed to say his name like that.

He responded with a surge of energy that sent her hand fluttering away from him in shocked surprise. He bit out something—a muttered curse, then the last scrap of silk was being taken away, trailing down pale, slender thighs that received the sharp, stinging touch of his kisses, kisses that began to work their way towards the one place they hadn't tasted yet.

'No,' she said. 'No.'

He didn't hear her. The first touch of his tongue lost her the will to protest. She groaned, she gasped, she shook and quivered. She clawed at his hair in a desperate effort to pull him away, then she wasn't pulling, she was stretching each wire-tight muscle as a new tension began to sing in her blood.

Hot, she felt hot. She felt bathed in static, the careful thrust of his fingers and the moist caress of his tongue dragging her on a silent scream towards a pinnacle she knew about but had never experienced.

'Oh, Carlo,' she whispered.

He moved over her in a single lithe, swift stretch of his body, claimed her mouth with a deep, hot, dark eroticism and at the same time made that first deep, penetrating thrust, seeking passage with a power that drove him through the fine barrier and locked her muscles on a pinprick cry of pain.

Stillness followed, a terrible silence. Her eyes flew open to stare up at him, he stared down, eyes turned black with shock. Between them the silken shaft of his penetration pulsated against the shock-contracted walls of her sheath and she waited, breath held, not sure if there was more pain to come or even if he was so appalled by his discovery that he was going to withdraw.

He didn't withdraw. He hissed out her name like a curse, flexed his tight buttocks then drove that bit deeper. Pain lost out to a scorching trail of agonising pleasure. His mouth trapped her aching gasps and her fingernails dug deep crescents into his chest. With each powerful, fiery thrust he possessed her that bit more, filled her, drove her towards a blank wall that she knew was going to burst apart and send her crashing into a devastating place. She was sobbing in fear of it yet desperate to get there. As if he understood, Carlo wrapped both arms beneath her and pressed his cheek to hers.

'Let go,' he said. That was all—let go—and she did, held tightly against him with his heated breath in her hair and his heartbeat pounding against her breasts, her sobs changing to gasps as she broke through the restraints holding her trapped to explode into a maelstrom of blistering ecstasy that jerked at her body and ripped at her breath and made Carlo lock her more tightly to him as he absorbed each quivering shockwave that dragged him shuddering into the same frenzied place.

She didn't think she was going to survive it. She really believed she was going to die. She closed her eyes and tried to decide whether that had been the most frightening experience of her life or the most beautiful. Nothing—nothing she'd ever heard or seen about the act of love with its culminate orgasm had prepared her for the devastating reality of it.

In a state of near complete shutdown, she actually had to tell herself to breathe. Carlo was breathing; he was heaving in breaths like a man who'd just completed a mile-long sprint. His body was wet with perspiration, hers was the same, and the heat the two of them were generating as he continued to hold her clamped to him was enough to turn to steam.

And the aftershocks were still attacking his body, his possession still an aggressive entity she could feel, while she was so weak and limp she couldn't move a single thing. Eventually he recovered enough to relax his grip and allowed her to sink back into cool cotton. But even when he stayed heavy on top of her and began layering soft kisses on her face she could not find the energy to respond.

I'm not real any more, she thought hazily. I've left my body and I'm floating somewhere up there.

'You are wonderful,' Carlo's husky voice murmured. 'You are the most beautiful creature living on this earth.'

She tried a weak smile, but that was all she managed.

The brush of his lips feathered that smile. 'I am one lucky guy to be lying here with you now and you are one lucky woman to have me as your first lover…'

Ah, she mused sleepily, he wanted some feedback. He

wanted her to confirm what a great lover he was. 'You're wonderful,' she returned lazily.

'Mm,' he said, and moved just enough to remind her that the wonder of him wasn't over yet. 'So,' he said lightly, 'when are you going to marry me?'

CHAPTER EIGHT

MARRIAGE...? Francesca came alert as if someone had thrown a light switch. Her eyes shot open to stare into a smooth, dark, slightly mocking face.

'Since when did marriage come into this?' she tremored disbelievingly.

'Since the first time I set eyes on you.' He leant down to kiss her protruding bottom lip.

Heat seared a passage right down to her abdomen. To her shock she realised he still possessed her and with a stifled gasp she wriggled herself free and instantly discovered that when you detached yourself from an aroused man the sensations it caused were as life-grabbing as the sex!

'I'm not marrying you,' she declared in a husky, shivering voice she hoped he read as anger and not what it actually was. 'You must be joking.' Why would a man like him want to marry her? 'No way,' she added for good measure and wriggled the rest of herself free before he got different ideas about what happened next.

'You mean I am being jilted already? But this means I did not last as long as Batiste! I am stricken,' he announced. 'My ego is fatally wounded.'

'Not your heart, I notice,' Francesca muttered as she scrambled off the bed. 'And you can't jilt someone when there was never a relationship in the first place.'

'Ah, so you prefer to be romanced as you were by Batiste than overwhelmed by my unabated passion. You should have said, *cara*,' he drawled as she looked anxiously around for something to cover up her nakedness. 'I would have brought you champagne and flowers instead of simply my amazing prowess.'

She saw the red silk coverlet draping the corner of the bed and reached for it, trailing it from around a heavy wood bedpost. 'Is there no limit to your arrogance?'

'Not after what we just shared.'

He moved on the bed, stretching like a long, sleek, well-pampered and very satisfied cat. Francesca wrapped herself in exotic silk and hoped to goodness he hadn't seen the hectic flush that had mounted her skin.

'You were amazing,' he murmured as he relaxed again. 'To respond to me with such wonderful generosity and passion when it was your first time made two precious gifts you gave to me. I will cherish them always—*gratzi tanto amore*...'

'*Prego,*' she said, moving slender shoulders in response to the ripple of feeling that arrived with the husky intimacy in his voice. She had never been so aware of her own sexuality—never would have believed that she had it in her to respond the way that she had.

'It was special—take my word for it...'

'Is—is there a bathroom in here?' she quavered, sending her eyes on a hunted scan of the walls, looking for a door that would offer her some kind of escape.

'...Because my word is all you will ever have to go on,' he continued as if she hadn't spoken. 'I think I've told you before that I am very possessive of what belongs to me.'

'I do not belong to you!' she turned to flash at him then and just stared as the firelight struck a flame down the length of his body and licked the aggressive length of his penis.

She looked away—wildly as tiny muscles between her thighs began to pulse. This had to stop. It *had* to! What am I doing here? she asked herself, trembling and tingling and... 'I think I w-want to go h-home,' she heard herself stammer.

'Sorry, *cara*, but, like me, you are committed. *This* is your new home. Next week we will marry and make it official.'

'I'm in love with another man!' she threw at him in the

shrill voice of panic. 'Why would you want to marry me knowing that?'

'What has love got to do with it?' He thoroughly mocked the word. 'I want you here, in my bed. The fact that you have just shown how much you want to be in my bed makes your so-called love for another man pretty useless here, *cara*. So I advise you not to bother mentioning it again.'

'I do *not* want you!' she denied furiously, which was really stupid of her after what they'd just shared. 'Again...' she added as a weak tag-on.

Sardonic eyes studied the hectic flush in her face then slowly, lazily drifted all the way down her front. She trembled from tumbled hair to toenails. 'Those two tight little nipples pushing against the silk are talking to me,' he taunted softly.

Francesca looked down. 'Oh,' she gasped in horror when she saw what he was seeing and crossed her arms over her tingling breasts and turned to make a dash for the bedroom door, tripping over trailing silk in her haste to get away.

'Oh, no, you don't...'

He came off the bed like a striking cobra, moving so fast that she'd barely reached for the door handle when he'd closed his hands on her shoulders and spun her around.

'You will not run away this time, Francesca,' he said grimly. 'Your chance to escape from what is now set in stone is long gone.'

His eyes were glittering down at her and there was nothing languid about his grim stance now. He was all tense and cruel-looking—exciting as— 'I don't know what you're talking about,' she mumbled distractedly and she wished he would go and put on some clothes.

No chance. His grip tightened on her shoulders. 'I put my pride and my reputation on the line for you tonight in front of my business colleagues and my friends,' he explained.

'I didn't ask you to.'

'You didn't stop me either,' he countered. 'Do you honestly think that I went to that much trouble just for a hot night of sex with you?'

Francesca shrugged, lowering her eyes because that was more or less exactly what she'd thought.

His breath hissed out from between his teeth. 'This may come as a surprise to you, *cara*, but I don't need to work that hard to get a woman in my bed. They usually line up to wait their turn—and that is not my arrogance talking,' he said before she did. 'It is simply the truth. The fact that I rarely choose to avail myself of what is on offer is due to a healthy respect for myself and who I share my body with!'

He shared it with her—all of it with her.

'There was not a person there tonight that did not assume my motives were strictly honourable—or that plans for our marriage would be announced soon. The moment you stepped out of the Batistes' villa with me you made an agreement on those terms and you are not going to make me look a fool in front of all of Rome, by ducking out of it!'

'I did not agree to become your wife—or your lover for that matter!'

'You can also stop lying to yourself!' he rasped. 'You have been wanting me as your lover from the moment our eyes met at a set of traffic lights. I knew it. You refused to acknowledge it. Now, my sensational Francesca, you have no choice but to admit that we *both* are crazy with desire for each other!'

'That's not—'

His mouth came down, crushing the lie from her lips and sending a rush of feeling shooting down her quivered length. Her legs suddenly felt like electrified wire. She didn't know what she was doing; the kiss took her over so completely she even threw off the silk cover so she could wind her arms around his neck and press herself into the sense-savaging heat of his naked length. He accommodated her standing rock-solid on long bare feet and holding her against him while she arched and stretched and moved as she kissed him back in a turmoil of sensuous greed.

'Angelo had no idea what he passed on,' he muttered as he lifted his head. Glinting eyes shot a narrowed look into her dazed, desire-shot eyes. 'Or maybe he did,' he then added grimly. 'Maybe he knew you would be too hot for him to handle. Is that why he turned to your much more predictable flatmate, do you think?'

It was a cruel comment too far. Francesca responded by instinct, feeling as stunned as he was when her arm made a slicing arc through the air to land the flat of her palm against his face. She had never done anything like it in her entire life before. She didn't even know where it had come from. And now she was heaving and gasping and quivering for a different reason, because he was furious. It pulsed all around him like a physical thing. She stood with her spine pressing back against the door and her palm tingling accusingly while she awaited his response. The silence thundered—or was it her heartbeat? And while she waited, eyes wide, lips parted and trembling, she had to watch the marks of her fingers begin to slowly stand out on his lean cheek.

Then it came, and she let out a small cry as his hands arrived on her shoulders. With a jerk she found herself flattened against him again and this time his mouth came crashing down on hers with no wish to make the kiss anything but a punishment. She supposed she deserved it. In some small, floundering part of her head she knew she should not have hit him, but still this angry kiss that ground the inner tissue of her lips against her teeth was brutal by comparison.

Then she was released, thrust away so her spine made contact with the door again while he turned his back and stepped away. 'Thank your lucky stars that I am not the kind of man that slaps back,' he said harshly.

No, it would be beneath his dignity to slap a woman. He preferred to use a fierce ravaging as revenge. Lifting tentative fingers to her bruised lips, she found them hot and swollen. To her wary consternation he swung around to look at her. He lifted a hand. For a horrible moment she thought he was going to change his mind and slap her anyway.

'Please don't,' she whispered.

He released a tense sigh. The hand took hold of her hand, gently removing it from her lips so he could inspect the results for himself while she stared up at him through huge, helpless eyes and trembled and shook and felt her throat start to sting.

'I deserved the slap,' he said.

And as a final humiliation, she burst into tears. She had been fighting them off all evening, and now they swept through her on an unrestrained flood that made her give way so thoroughly she dropped into a puddle of flaming red silk, covered her face with her hands and sobbed for all she was worth.

Carlo felt as if he had been sliced open and gutted. He just had not expected it. Why had he not expected it? he demanded of himself as he stood in frozen stillness, watching her fall apart in front of him. She had taken so many blows tonight that it was inevitable that one of them had to be the final blow.

The fact that it was his ruthless blow that had caused her breakdown dragged out his conscience so he had to stare it full in the face. He felt his mouth work in a tense quiver. A thick lump arrived in his throat. On a self-condemning curse he bent to lift her back to her feet, bringing the red cover up with her and engulfing her in it before wrapping her against him.

'Francesca—*amore*, I'm sorry,' he murmured huskily. 'Don't.'

'I h-hate you,' she sobbed.

'*Sì*,' he agreed with a touch of unsteadiness. 'I am a monster. Shout at me. Slap my face. But don't weep; I'm not worth it.'

For some reason this low opinion of himself made her

weep all the harder. 'I don't know what's happening to me!' she cried against his throat.

'No.' He could understand that. The whole evening had run like a black comedy for her. If she hadn't had enough to deal with tonight with the betrayal of both her fiancé and her best friend, she'd had to deal with his anger, his vile-humoured mockery, his bloody single-minded seduction that robbed her of her innocence, and finally—his contempt.

What did that say about him?

He didn't want to hear the answer to that—he didn't think his ego could take it right now.

She was trembling and sobbing against him; the scent permeating from her body smelled of him. He went to utter yet another apology then pinned his lips together because he couldn't trust them to say the right thing. So he went for the practical gesture of contrition, bent to place an arm behind her knees and scooped her up in his arms.

The bed looked tempting but he bypassed it, carrying her into the bathroom, where he set her down on the bath stool then left her there to weep while he turned and with a touch to a hi-tech switch set water gushing into the spa bathtub that took up almost half the space in the room. Next he hooked up a towel and draped it around his hips—hiding, he mused with a grimace.

Francesca was still weeping softly into her exotic silk shroud, her hair a tumble of loose, dark golden spirals that covered her face. He went to squat down in front of her then silently handed her a cloth for her tears. Taking it required her to expose a delicate pale shoulder to set free an arm and a hand. Her slender fingers were trembling as she took the cloth from him and her muffled, 'Thank you,' twisted his heart.

She used the cloth to mop up her eyes. 'Sorry,' she said though he didn't know why she did.

'Don't apologise to me, Francesca,' he said soberly. 'I think the tears were well overdue.'

'You've tied m-me in knots.'

'*Sì,*' he accepted.

'You've pl-played me like a puppet on strings.'

'*Sì,*' he agreed again, but this time it came with a wry smile. 'Great strings though, *cara*,' he could not resist saying. 'Wonderfully passionate and responsive strings.'

She heaved in a shaky breath of air. 'Stop talking like that,' she said, and pressed the cloth to her eyes. 'H-have you no guilty conscience?'

'About making love with you? None at all.' Which was the truth.

'Well, you should.'

'Because I want you?' he said, watching the careful way she kept her face averted from him. 'Because I am willing to do anything to keep you here with me?'

'Which says what you want—n-not what I want.'

'And what do you want?' he questioned gently.

How was she supposed to answer that when the whole point was that she didn't know? Francesca thought painfully. She was so confused and fearful because she didn't feel in control of herself any more. Shocked too, because she'd discovered that she had the ability to turn into an absolute raving sex wanton and—more awful—loved feeling that way.

How was it possible that she could feel anything like this when she was supposed to be breaking her heart over another man?

Oh, God, she groaned silently, feeling the light touch of his hand brush her tumbled hair from her damp cheek, and made the big mistake of lifting her face to look at him.

It was like walking head-on into the answer to everything.

Him. Signor Carlo Carlucci—her lover. The rush of feeling the title evoked robbed her of the ability to breathe. His hair was tousled and his cheek still wore the remnants of her fingers against it. The anger had gone from his eyes but not the passion; that still lingered in the low burn she could just see glimmering behind the dark.

His shoulders were bare, as was his long torso, and the rest of him was hidden by a towel that was doing so little to stop a rush of awareness from attacking her because of the way he was squatting with his thighs spread, parting the towel enough for her to be aware of what was lurking there.

'Don't start weeping again,' he said as he watched her eyes begin to fill. 'Tears will gain you no sympathy from me because I have discovered I like them.' He even reached out to brush a teardrop from the corner of her eye as it spilled onto her cheek. 'They may make you feel vulnerable and weak but they make me feel very protective and tough.'

'Mr Macho,' she mocked, making a play of using the cloth to wipe her eyes again but really she was trying to wipe away the tingling his gentle touch had left behind.

'*Sì,*' he agreed. 'You cry like a baby yet I don't see a single unsightly red blemish spoiling your beautiful pale face.'

'What has that got to do with anything?'

'It makes you special,' he said. 'I have never seen a woman cry without ruining her looks. I might decide to make you cry often because I love the huge pools of ocean-green your eyes have become.'

'My eyes aren't green, they're hazel.'

He ignored the correction. 'They make me want to drown in them. They make me want to gather you in my arms and kiss your worries away.'

And he was doing it again, seducing her with the honeyed tone of his voice, using passion for persuasion and words with which to beat her defences to death.

'You're my major worry.'

'Why?'

'Because you make me want you when I don't want to want you!'

There, she'd said it. Put the whole wretched problem in one neat sentence. She wanted him but didn't want to want him! Good grief, but it felt good to have a sensible label she could stick on all of this.

'Ah,' was all he said and climbed to his feet.

But the way he said that made her look up to study his smooth, handsome face. 'What was that supposed to mean?' she asked warily.

'Nothing,' he said and turned to switch off the flood of water pouring into the huge bath. Another switch was hit. A bubbling sound burst into life. Subtle aromas began teasing her nostrils with the sensual hint of aromatic oils captured in spirals of steam that rose up against a background of sumptuous red and black-grained marble surrounding the biggest spa bathtub she had ever seen in her life.

Then her attention was quickly grabbed back by him when the towel around his hips was dropped. She caught a glimpse of a lean, tanned, muscle-tight behind just before he turned around and faced her with the full force of the man she had met in the bedroom.

He was fully aroused. Her senses gave a shuddering throb, her eyes leaping up to the savage beauty of his face— as her alerted senses were now seeing him anyway.

'N-no,' she gasped.

It was the only protest she managed before he bent, kissed her mouth and deftly robbed her of the silk cover then lifted her back into his arms. Her second protest was ignored when he turned, stepped into the bath then sat down and repositioned her to sit between his spread thighs. Delicately fragranced blood-hot water bubbled up all around her; she felt the gloss of aromatic oils cling to her skin. With the movements of a man possessed of supreme self-confidence, he eased her rigid spine to curve into him.

'Relax,' he lowered his mouth to her ear to murmur. 'Enjoy your second new experience of the night.'

'You can't—'

'Oh, I can,' he assured her lazily. 'But I won't—not yet anyway. I was referring to the water, *cara*, and what it feels like to be washed by a man…'

He did in the end. It was inevitable, Francesca thought hours later as she lay watching the dawn break the night sky. What had begun as his determined assault on her senses while he was supposed to remain sublimely in control, ended up with her straddling his lap, making love with a man who didn't mind that she saw how deeply she could affect him.

Their third experience took place in bed—only not the bed they had first shared but—his bed. His bed. The one he had brought her to after the bath. It came as a shock to realise that he hadn't deliberately set out to seduce her that night.

'I do have scruples,' he'd smiled at the expressive look on her face. 'I did intend to give you a few days to recover from your ordeal by Batiste, but events overtook scruples.' He'd shrugged.

So here she lay in a room with soft cream walls and a huge, very modern divan bed with its snowy white cotton coverlet sliding off the corner of the bed. Everything in the room was either cream or white, though the floor was the same beautifully polished wood.

She preferred him in the red-room setting, she decided as she lay there. All the fire and passion the room evoked suited his temperament.

Or had the other room been chosen because he'd thought it suited her temperament? It did strange things to her to think that he saw her as the exotic wanton she'd become in his arms.

Turning her head on the pillow, she looked at him. He was lying on his stomach and sound asleep, but had an arm curved possessively around her as if he was making sure she didn't go anywhere while he snatched a few hours' respite.

He had, in a few short hours, shattered every principle by which she'd lived and the awful part was that she no longer cared, so maybe he was the perceptive one and she the closet wanton who'd spent years of adulthood lying to herself.

Or hiding from herself, she then amended, thinking of all those other men she'd held off with ease as if some inner instinct had held her back from allowing the real Francesca to reveal herself—until this man came along.

This strong, dark, beautiful man with the kind of passions her instincts had recognised would match her own. So they'd unlocked their restraints and set the real Francesca free to indulge every sensual desire she possessed.

She'd told herself that she wanted to wake this morning as a different woman and she had. His woman. She didn't even bother to argue with that any more.

He stirred in his sleep, his mouth brushing against her shoulder as he moved. She looked at his mouth, traced its shape with her eyes and felt the impact of its passion on just about every inch of her skin. A sigh whispered from her. It sounded sensuously languorous. But then everything about her was like that now. She looked, felt and was sensuously languorous. She liked it. She even turned carefully so as not to waken him and brushed her kiss against his shoulder before she curled against him, closed her eyes and drifted into sensual sleep.

Lying beside her, propped up on an elbow, Carlo watched her come slowly awake. He was helping the gentle swim up from her little dream world, of course, by the slow, light circling of her nipple with a finger. The rosebud tip was already invitingly erect and he was going to lower his head and enjoy it in a moment. But for now he was content to enjoy watching her respond without being aware that she was doing it with her soft, feathered breathing that turned on his senses and the way the rest of her body was making some very seductive undulating movements.

He watched as her lips parted, felt the heavy tow of desire begin to creep through his blood. He'd never known a woman like her. If asked, until last night, he would have stated that virginity was nothing more than an obstacle that must be surmounted before the real enjoyment could begin. Not so, he knew now. Virginity meant innocence—for Francesca anyway. And her innocence was a like a blank canvas on which he was free to paint whatever colourful impressions he wished to create.

Her breathtaking willingness to trust his guidance through all things to do with sensual pleasure being the richest colour he was painting with. It was an empowering experience, and yet another gift she had given him.

Dangerous, he thought. Very dangerous if entrusted to the wrong man. Batiste, for instance—how would he have treated this precious gift if she had given it to him?

Then—no. He shut that thought away when his senses began to tighten just thinking of Batiste touching her like this. Any other man, he then expanded jealously. Francesca belonged to him and the sooner she came to terms with that the better it was going to be for both of them.

She didn't want to want him.

He smiled as he recalled those telling words. Well, *cara*, he told her silently, by the time the next few days are over I am going to turn that statement on its head.

He began by closing his mouth around his prepared prize, his eyes still fixed on her face to watch her response. Her eyelashes fluttered. He moved his tongue. She released a small, very sexy sigh. He sucked delicately. She arched her slender spine towards the source of her pleasure and relaxed again then slowly opened her eyes.

'Ciao,' he said softly and snaked up to steal a kiss from her sleep-softened, beautiful mouth. She clung very satisfyingly but when he lifted his head again he saw the wariness was already creeping in.

'I…'

'*We* are going to enjoy an—interesting day today,' he layered lightly over whatever she had been going to say.

'You...'

'And *we* are going to begin it as all perfect days should begin, with some very slow loving.'

He grinned rakishly then lowered his head again—to the inviting nipple waiting for him.

And so continued the ravishment of Francesca Bernard, Francesca acknowledged as she fell into his honeyed trap without putting up much resistance at all. He ravished her with his body and with his easy charm. When they eventually went down to find some breakfast he ravished her on the terrace with warm, needy looks across a sunny breakfast table overlooking a sparkling lake.

She discovered that Lorenzo had a wife called Caprice and between the two of them they looked after the house. They didn't live in. They had a villa of their own situated in a sunny corner of the grounds and had two sons that looked after the extensive gardens that curled horseshoe-like around the *palazzo*.

Carlo showed her the *palazzo*, and ravished her with the rich, melodious tones of his voice as he displayed his intimate knowledge of the *palazzo*'s amazing history and of his ancestors, each of whom had left their mark here over the centuries. She hung on every warmly informative word like a mesmerised cat and let him make love to her in the humid warmth of the solarium, on a chaise tucked inside a jungle of exotic tropical foliage.

'Trust me,' was his favourite answer to any hesitation she might reveal in the process of making love. 'Trust me, you will love this. Trust me, I can make this wonderful for you.'

And he did, every time. She learnt things about herself—and things about him that could swamp her mind when she allowed herself to think about them afterwards. He touched her at every given opportunity. If he couldn't touch he made love to her with his eyes. He kept her balanced on a needle-sharp tip of sensual awareness that never let up—even when she slept.

If she slept. One day drifted into two then three, and sleep had become a snatched thing she did between sensual assaults. He was insatiable, devastatingly inventive and—shocking.

Sometimes.

Sometimes he fell so thoroughly into her power that she became the shocking one.

They didn't leave the *palazzo*. They didn't talk about the things that they should. If she tried to broach the subject of reality he stalled her with, 'Don't spoil it, *cara*. Trust me, it will turn into a fight.'

Living in this unreal, cloistered little world he had carefully wrapped her in was foolish. In those few moments before sleep she'd sometimes find herself wondering if this was a deliberate campaign he was waging to soften her up for a ruthless kill.

Sometimes. Most of the time she didn't want to think at all. Especially if thinking meant facing head-on the issues they'd both pushed to one side.

Like his marriage proposal for instance; that still made no sense to her whatever way he chose to dress it up. And, as with each new experience another veil of innocence was taken from her, she had to question why she was letting this happen at all.

She'd even said out loud to him, 'I don't know why I'm letting you do this to me.'

'Why think at all?' had come his light response. 'Why not just enjoy?'

Because it wasn't that easy, she thought with a frown as she sat on one of the lichen-dressed stone benches against a high stone wall that formed one of the many terraces which swept the garden down towards the lake.

For once she'd escaped his almost constant presence while he dealt with a business call in his study-cum-office inside the house. The respite was giving her a chance to do the one thing he'd advised against her doing—and that was to think.

She'd gone from loving one man to becoming sexually obsessed with another in the same time it took to think the words. She didn't think she liked what that said about her. In fact she knew that she didn't. Putting her life on hold like this was solving nothing and they couldn't go on much longer without the world trying to intrude on their sensual retreat. He was already receiving a string of business calls that demanded his attention and reminded them both that he had a multinational business to run, while she had...

Nothing.

No life left out there to make her want to return to it. No friends left she felt she could trust. Not even a great-uncle she wanted to go on hoping would soften his hard stance towards her.

All she had left to cling to, in other words, was—him.

As if he knew what she was thinking he suddenly appeared, striding along the pathway between the wall and the spread of freshly mown turf, which led to the edge of the next terrace drop. It was like watching sheer poetry in motion, she thought as she followed the long, graceful stretch of his stride and the way the sun on his hair was making her think of ravens' wings again. She looked away—quickly—and began frowning out at the lake again.

He sat down beside her and stretched out those long legs in front of him. 'Calculating how quickly these gardens could be turned into a wilderness?' he said lightly.

CHAPTER NINE

'THE gardens are lovely as they are and you know it,' she answered quietly.

'But they do not inspire you to defend them with passion like the Palazzo Gianni,' he sighed with teasing regret.

Mention of her great-uncle's home froze her up so quickly that she even shivered. 'The Palazzo Gianni is a dump and a ruin.'

'But a dump and a ruin with soul and atmosphere,' he promptly extended. 'Perhaps we could allow the west terrace to revert back to nature so you can feel the same blood rush of passion…'

'I would rather not be reminded of what I said back then when I was blind and stupid, thank you,' she cut in with a snap and got up to walk a few tense steps away, aware that her abrupt change in mood had left him sitting there frowning at her in surprise.

'Would you like to explain the reason for this little outburst?' he requested eventually.

'I just don't want to be reminded of the Palazzo Gianni,' she supplied.

'But your great-uncle—'

'Has gone on my special discarded heap of people I no longer wish to associate with.'

The space behind her was filled with grim silence. She was already regretting her irritable snap but did not seem able to push this new restlessness away again. She turned to glance at him. She was wearing her denims and her hair was up. He was wearing denims too but the outfit looked a whole lot more sexy on him. The black hair, the olive-toned skin, the way he was sitting with his legs stretched out and his arms resting along the back of the stone seat. He was still frowning and even that was sexy.

'Who else is on this heap?' he questioned.

'Angelo; Sonya.' She effected a shrug. 'Anyone else from now on who thinks they can play around with my feelings and get away with it.'

'Growing tough, hm?'

'Yes.' She frowned at her black-booted feet. 'I've discovered I have more Gianni blood than I thought I had,' she then added bleakly. 'There wasn't a forgiving bone in any Gianni I've ever heard about. They just severed connection with those people that let them down and that's it, problem solved, you can't be hurt by those who don't exist any more. Great way to deal with life.' She tossed up her head to stare bleakly at the lake. 'I'm going to cultivate it.'

'And Bruno Gianni deserves this brutal—severing?'

'Oh, yes.' She nodded, then took in a deep breath and explained to him about her one and only meeting with Bruno Gianni. She told him what she'd said, what he'd said and about all her ensuing letters to him that had been coldly ignored. 'He sees me as Maria Bernard's shame-child. Like my mother, I don't exist, in other words. Well, that's fine by me because he doesn't exist for me any more.'

'But Bruno is your only living relative, Francesca. You cannot really want to cut him out of your life without giving him a chance to—'

'To what?' she challenged. 'Come round? Soften his miserable stance and condescend to accept me? Be careful, Carlo,' she cautioned acidly, 'or I might start to wonder if you're no better than Angelo.'

Her eyes gave a bitter flash. His narrowed, glinting at her in the afternoon sun. 'Meaning what?' he demanded.

He hadn't moved a single muscle but Francesca suddenly felt as if she was treading on unstable ground.

'Nothing,' she said, backing down from the brewing fight. But Carlo was not going to let her do that. 'Oh, don't

stop with nothing, *cara*,' he drawled. 'I am now totally riv-
eted by the conversation. In what way am I being compared
to Batiste?'

Defiance made her lift her chin to him. 'You might think
you have me all wrapped up and labelled—yours for the
taking—but you're wrong, Carlo. I still have enough brain
left to question why you are doing all of this.'

'We've been through that.' He frowned.

'Have we?' she disputed. 'The way I recall it, you did a
lot of telling me what we were going to do and I did a lot
of protesting, which you arrogantly ignored. Since then we
have hidden away here like a pair of clandestine lovers doing lots of sex but nothing much else—while Rome, I pre-
sume, waits with bated breath to see what Carlo Carlucci
does next with the Gianni heiress.'

She came to a teeth-snapping silence, inwardly stunned
by how much she'd needed to say all of that. Carlo did
nothing. He just continued to sit there staring at her with
his thoughts locked away behind those narrowed eyes.

'All of Rome, hm?' he murmured then. 'Interesting, *cara*,
but it avoids the question as to what way I am being compared to Batiste.'

Lips pinned shut, she refused to answer. The silence
gnawed like teeth on bone. In the end he said what she
refused to say out loud—was too scared to say in case
speaking the words filled them with a wretched ring of truth.

'You think I am just another fortune-hunter like Batiste,
solely after your family's secret stash.'

'Well—are you?' she flashed.

He moved at last and her heart took on a hectic flurry as
he folded his arms across his chest, crossed his long
stretched-out legs and proceeded to study her with a smooth,
sleek, unfathomable assessment of a man taking his time
considering his answer before he spoke.

Was he angry? She couldn't tell but she knew suddenly
that she was looking at the tough businessman she'd heard

about but never seen before with her own eyes. She didn't think she liked him. In fact she was sure that she didn't—so much so that she thought about running again before he made up his mind how to answer...then changed her mind.

No, she thought. It was time that they dealt with this. And there was no way she was going to let him intimidate her with that look. So she folded her own arms beneath her breasts and lifted her chin that bit higher to give him back glinting look for look. Something new filtered into the atmosphere—a taste for a fight. It had a rather sexy hint to it that tingled through her blood—more so when he opened his mouth to speak.

'For every Gianni euro you put on the table I will match it with a million euro,' he announced.

It was a smooth, slick throwing-down of the gauntlet. But more than that, it had taken her by surprise. A million? she was reluctantly impressed. His remarks the other evening about the Gianni fortune being able to buy out half of Rome made his fortune obscenely large indeed. 'Now, that's an awful lot of money,' she conceded.

He smiled—thinly. 'Nothing multiplied by nothing is—nothing, *cara*. So don't start counting it quite yet.' Then he smiled. 'Though I will allow you to be impressed.'

'I am,' she admitted. 'So why do these very impressive millions want to attach themselves to me?'

'Billions,' he corrected. 'I am a fabulously wealthy man, my sweet-tongued angel. Look around you and check out the Carlucci credentials if you don't believe me. Though I was hoping that my—charm alone would have been enough to say I am worthy husband material for a *half* Gianni with nothing but her suspicious self to offer me.'

He was—a billion times more than enough for her. And that, she thought bleakly, was the crux of the problem she was struggling with. Four nights ago she had been in love with Angelo; today, as she stood here in the bright sunlight looking into his handsome face, she knew—almost knew—that today she was in love with Carlo.

Fickle didn't come close to describing how that made her view herself. She just had to start mistrusting her ability to know how she felt about anything any more. And while she felt like this…

'I feel as if Francesca Bernard died that night of her betrothal party and this—person I've become is such a complete stranger to me that she needs a new name,' she murmured helplessly.

'I can give you a new name. Marry me and become Francesca Carlucci.'

Just like that. He made it sound so simple but—she shook her head. 'I won't marry you, Carlo,' she told him huskily.

He responded with—nothing.

She twitched restlessly. 'Why bother with marriage at all?' she asked. 'You don't need to marry me; I'll stay around without the ring.'

She could hardly say otherwise after the way she'd been responding to him. She was in too deep and that worried her too.

'As my mistress.'

'As your *anything*!' She rounded on him agitatedly. 'Except your wife.'

He stared at her for a few moments longer, no smile, no noticeable change in him anywhere to give her fair warning of what was about to come.

'Then it's nothing,' he announced, got up and walked away, leaving her standing there frozen in shock at the clean, cold way he had made that decision!

But her heart wasn't frozen, it began to beat wildly, a sudden deep, thick ball of stark panic rising up in her throat. He didn't mean it, she told herself. He was just trying to pay her back for turning his offer down the way she had.

Thinking that didn't stop her from suddenly taking off after him though. *Believing* it didn't stop her from racing up the shallow layers of wide steps with the anxious intent to seek him out.

He was already inside the house by the time she shot beneath one of the elegant archways that framed the lake. Entering the house at a run she took the stairs, and was running down the upper corridor when a sound outside the windows brought her to a shuddering halt.

Glancing out of the window, she saw Carlo standing in the courtyard talking to Lorenzo. He looked his usual cool self, supremely relaxed, the sunlight catching his hair again and the olive sheen of his skin as he talked. There was no sign at all that he had just made the most momentous decision of their very brief relationship.

It's OK, she calmed herself. He had just been bluffing her—playing the smooth, slick manipulator to the wretched hilt.

She took in a deep breath, let it out again, blamed the breathless feeling on her mad run and was about to turn away and walk *calmly* into their bedroom—when he raised a hand to make a gesture as he talked, and she saw a flash of something metallic glint in his hand.

Car keys.

The panic rose again and so swiftly she didn't even have to think before it had enveloped her.

He was going to go.

He was going to get in his car and drive away.

He was probably telling Lorenzo to get rid of her while he was gone!

He was ruthless, heartless. She'd probably let what bit of conscience he had off the hook when she'd turned his proposal down and now he was striding towards his car as if a huge great weight had been lifted from his shoulders!

And she should let him go.

But she didn't let him go. She hit the stairs at a sprint and all but slithered her way down them to the ground floor.

She couldn't breathe, yet she was panting like a maniac. She ran along the hall and pulled open the front door.

The car was just reversing from beneath its shady parking spot beneath an old olive tree. Her head was spinning; she didn't even know what she was doing as she sprinted at an angle across uneven cobblestones and reached the car as it paused in its manoeuvre, facing the gates, waiting for them to open.

Her fingers fumbled with the door catch. She tugged open the door and sent it flying wide. 'No, don't go,' she said in a dark, thick, husky tremor. 'Don't leave me here.'

Then was launching herself into the car and onto his surprised lap. Her ribs grazed painfully against the steering wheel but she didn't care; her arms flew tightly around his neck.

'I'll marry you. I'll do anything—h-hide in your bed! Just don't—'

At which point she burst into sobbing tears.

Carlo had never been more stunned by anything than to have her weep all over him again. Reaching out with a hand, he switched off the car's ignition then sat back. Her arms were gripping his neck like a vice, her body heaving, her hot tears drenching his throat.

'This is very innovative of you, *cara*, he murmured, 'but the tears are a bit over-the-top.'

'Y-you don't understand,' she sobbed. 'I don't like m-myself any more.'

'No.' He was beginning to see that.

'Y-you use me—*they* u-used me and I just let you all do it!'

'We will leave other people out of this, I think.' His hands went up to frame her face so he could lift it out of its hiding place; she looked so pathetic he wanted to kiss her so badly he ached. 'But how do I use you?' he challenged sternly. 'And don't dare quote the sex at me,' he warned, 'because

I am the sex slave around here. Your every sensual wish has been my command!'

'That's not true!' Her eyes were so big and tear-soaked he wanted to drown in them again. He did the next best thing and kissed her hard. She responded as she always did, with heat and verve and some heart-rending sobs thrown in.

'The born sensualist and the sex slave—the perfect combination,' he muttered as he drew away again. 'Forget the marriage thing, Francesca. I think we are perfect as we are. So, come on...'

Before she could respond he tipped her off his lap and out of the car onto the courtyard so that he could get out of the car.

'But...' She'd changed her mind. Well, tough, *cara*, he thought.

'The offer,' he incised, 'has been closed.'

She looked so wounded he wanted to hit something—the car was closest. He slammed the door then took her hand.

'Where were you going?' she asked as he began pulling her behind him back to the house.

'It is of no importance now,' he answered blandly, feeling as ruthless as hell. Why tell her that he had been on his way to deal with the whole Gianni situation once and for all? 'What does matter now is that we are going to play this your way. We will go inside and pack then get back to Rome, where you will hide in my bed and I will indulge your every fantasy because that, *cara*, is my role...'

He drove them to Rome with the same single-minded, typically Italian daring and panache that he'd driven her away from Villa Batiste a few nights before. He didn't speak and neither did Francesca. She wasn't happy but she didn't know why she wasn't happy when he'd conceded to her every wish.

Contrary is what you are, she told herself glumly. You

want one thing then when you are given it you start wondering if you prefer what it is you turned down!

Maybe it was Carlo Carlucci, the whole package, that was her real problem. Maybe she should have let him leave when he was going to do it without her, instead of falling on him like the plague.

Oh… She shuddered, shifting restlessly at her own awful description.

'Almost there,' his quiet voice murmured as if she was a restless child that needed soothing—and that irritated her too.

He turned beneath an archway, which opened up into another enclosed courtyard, and slotted the car into a parking space between lines of cars that wore their wealth as much as the three-storey buildings that said exclusive city living to her. As she got out of the car she recognised her Vespa parked neatly against a wall.

'I had it delivered,' he explained, following her gaze then arching a challenging smile at her when she frowned.

They entered through a door and climbed the stairs to the top floor. The apartment was huge, spreading across two corners of the building. She wandered aimlessly from room to room while Carlo dealt with a stack of mail that had been waiting for him on a table in the foyer. His eyes followed her though, flicking her lowered glances as she wandered out of one room to move to the next. She spied all her stuff from her flat stacked in what looked like a spare bedroom by its small size—in comparison to the two other large, luxurious bedrooms she'd already checked out, along with the luxurious sitting room, a fabulous formal dining room, a very male study and a kitchen that was bigger than the whole area of her apartment.

'How did these get here?' she asked him.

'Your—friend packed them for you,' he replied.

'When did she pack them?'

He made a play of slotting a letter back in its envelope before saying casually, 'The day after we left Villa Batiste.'

He was that sure she was going to end up here with him at some point? 'I suppose my nightdress is already laid out on your bed,' she said.

'Since you know you won't be wearing such a garment in my bed, *cara*, you can quit the sarcasm and tell me what you think.'

'Are you joking? It's gorgeous and you know it.' The city apartment for the city-slick sophisticate. 'Is that Canaletto hanging in the sitting room the original or a fake?'

He lost interest in the letters. 'What's the matter with you?' He frowned.

Besides feeling as if I'd won the battle but lost the war? 'I wish I knew.' She shrugged. 'I feel as if I've stepped out of fairy-tale history straight into the perfect example of its modern-day equivalent.'

'But the handsome rake who intends to ravish you is still the same guy, *mi amante*...'

Her skin began to prickle, sending warning signals to her legs as the letters slipped from his open fingers to land on the table and the gleam in his eyes said—

With a shriek of protest she turned and made a bolt for it. It was her misfortune that she chose to run into the room that she did. His flying tackle carried her with ease onto the middle of the big, downy, soft bed. After that she didn't care where they were as they fought and tumbled and made love until the sky began to darken and hunger pangs began to strike.

It was after they'd showered and he'd suggested that they get dressed and go out to find something to eat that she remembered she didn't have anything to wear because all her clothes were stuffed away in boxes or in the suitcase still languishing in his car boot.

With his usual casual manner he strode naked across the bedroom, pulled open a door and silently gestured her to take a look inside. What she saw was rail upon rail of the most fantastic clothes she had ever seen in her life.

'For me?' she gasped in disbelief.

'Who else shares my bedroom with me?' he mocked lightly.

'But I will never wear all of these!'

'Try,' he suggested, kissed her cheek and strode off to the opposite side of the room towards a door.

'Carlo…' The call of his name stayed him as he reached for the door handle and he half turned to look at her. 'Thank you,' she said softly. 'But you don't have to buy me things. I can—'

'I know,' he cut in gently. 'It gave me pleasure, *cara mia*. Accept, enjoy—and choose something to drive me crazy while we eat!' was his last comment before he disappeared from view.

She chose a pale, misty purple wrap-over dress that scooped low between her breasts and was held together by nothing more than a couple of strategically placed hooks and eyes. And because she wasn't quite brave enough to go out wearing such a wickedly sexy creation she added a long-sleeved sheer chiffon blouse in the same misty colour patterned with scrolls of cloud-grey. She put her hair up, slipped her feet into a pair of backless shoes then stepped out of her exotic new dressing room to find the man of her dreams waiting for her.

He was wearing a casual suit made of taupe linen and a dark blue open-necked shirt and he looked so attractive her breathing stilled. His eyes darkened as they drifted over her, the sensual curve of his eyelids touching his chiselled cheeks.

'Now, that is most definitely risky,' he drawled lazily and made her blush, which made him grin.

They walked the short way to a local restaurant he told her was a favourite of his and seduced each other beneath soft lighting across the dinner table while they ate food neither of them noticed. It was all very bewitching. Francesca began to see them truly as lovers for the first time since their intimacy had begun.

Then two couples came in, saw Carlo and came over to their table to say hello. Francesca could not have repeated their names afterwards, only the way Carlo introduced her as 'my lover, Francesca', and the curious looks she received, which made her aware of her name and her notoriety.

They were nice people though, too well brought up and refined to stare for too long or ask awkward questions. They joined them for a glass of wine and she actually found herself relaxing with them. And all the time that they sat there talking and laughing, Carlo's hand never relinquished its hold on hers.

As he watched the wary tension slowly seeping out of her, Carlo wondered if she had any idea how beautiful and beguiling she looked when she used that shy and tentative smile on his friends.

When they left the others to enjoy their meal and began the walk back to his apartment, he drew her beneath the wrap of his arm and felt her hand slide up beneath his jacket to come to rest between his shoulder blades. They fitted each other in every way a pair of lovers could do, he noted. Then frowned because *lovers*, was not the label he wanted them to share. It was all such a damn mess, he thought grimly. But how the hell he was going to sort it out without hurting her he had no idea at the present moment.

'Why the sigh?' She lifted her face to look up at him.

He lowered his to steal a kiss. 'You're too beautiful,' he replied. 'I was considering whether to keep you hidden in my bed in future as we agreed instead of risking you out here, where there are other men to turn your head.'

She laughed, it was a gorgeous sound, soft and light yet unbelievably sensual. 'Modesty isn't your thing, *caro*,' she told him drily. 'You know that I know I'm already with the best.'

'*Gratzi.*'

'*Prego.*'

He pulled her into a darkened shop doorway. 'You are becoming too big for your dainty shoes,' he scolded. 'I think it is time you were reminded who is the boss around this relationship.'

Then he kissed her until she begged him to stop. Until she agreed—breathlessly, 'OK, you're the boss,' and he took her home to substantiate it with more—physical methods.

It was a role he filled to its optimum capacity, Francesca mused as she walked through the apartment that had come to feel like home to her after living here with Carlo for several wonderful weeks.

In fact the only cloud on their sunny horizon was her insistence that she was going back to work and his disapproval of her doing it. They'd had a really big row about it when the subject came up. She had won—mainly because, having gone into the office to hand in her resignation, she'd ended up giving in to Bianca's pleading. It was high season and the tourist industry was at the height of its flood. Sonya had apparently returned to England, which had left Bianca short of two guides. She'd apologised for not telling Francesca that she'd suspected that Angelo was Sonya's other man.

'How do you break that kind of news to someone when it is only a suspicion?' she'd said.

With a bit more cajoling and the knowledge that Francesca was already bored, kicking her heels on her own throughout the day while Carlo went about his high-powered business, Bianca had gleaned a promise out of her that she would continue with her job.

So she spent her days back in her red uniform, being the efficient tour guide, and came home in the evenings to change into the clothes Carlo had bought to become his attentive lover.

No man could have it any better. No woman could want for more. Carlo eased them gently into socialising by carefully picking those close friends and associates who did not move in the same social circles as the Batistes.

He continued to introduce her as 'my lover, Francesca', and in a tone that demanded she be judged on the value he placed on her in that role. And, since it was well known that he'd literally scythed her away from Angelo on the night of their engagement, that value meant a great deal—or so she let herself believe.

He rarely left her side on these occasions; he made no effort to conceal she did things for him that kept him faithfully at heel. She blossomed under this kind of devotion, and even learned to tease him by flirting once or twice just to watch his eyes darken and read the threat of what her punishment would be.

She also learned to value herself again—learned slowly to trust him.

Then she met Angelo.

They were attending a charity function in one of the big city hotels and had been there for about an hour when she detached herself from Carlo's side to go and find the ladies' room. It was as she was walking back into the main reception room that she walked straight into Angelo. If she'd known he was here she would have been on her guard and therefore avoided this kind of face-to-face confrontation but the way it happened the two of them just stood staring at each other in a surprised and discomforted silence.

He looked as he always did—the beautifully turned-out, handsome guy, still with that golden glow about him which had blinded her to the real man. The charm was missing though, she noticed as she looked into his blue eyes and saw no false warmth or perpetual smile lurking around his mouth.

A nerve twitched in his jaw as he skimmed his eyes over her tight little strapless dress made of pale peach satin that moulded her figure like a second skin. Her hair had been cut to highlight the natural streaks of gold in the light brown, and expertly styled to float around her heart-shaped face and slender shoulders. She knew she looked good because Carlo had told her so—in more ways than one.

But she did not need Angelo confirming that judgement. 'You look amazing,' he said curtly. 'I will give it to Carlucci—he has managed to bring out the best in you.'

Tension spun a steely case around her throat because she didn't want him looking at her like that—with lying eyes that pretended to desire what they saw.

'I have nothing to say to you—excuse me,' she said and went to walk past him.

His hand captured hers, bringing her to a halt shoulder to shoulder with him. She fixed her eyes on the milling throng, anxiously checking out how many people had noticed them standing here.

'Let me go,' she insisted.

'Not until you have heard me out.' His grip tightened on her fingers. 'What you overheard me say to Sonya that night about not wanting you was all lies, Francesca. The kind of lies any aroused man will utter without conscience to keep the woman in his arms sweet.'

'Is telling me that supposed to make me feel better about you?' she asked.

'No,' he said. 'But it does me a lot of good to let you know that I was never blind to your attractions, *cara*. I wanted you. It was you who tied my hands with your shy confessions of innocence and old-fashioned views on marriage before sex. I can't tell you how bloody annoying it is to know that if I'd pushed the issue as Carlucci obviously has, then Sonya would not have got a look-in and we would be standing here as a happily married couple now.'

'You believe a marriage based on your desire to get your

hands on Gianni money could be happy?' She pushed out a derogatory laugh. 'By now, *caro,* you would know there is no money and be as unhappy as a greedy man with no fortune to spend could be.'

'So you are still sticking to the no-fortune story,' he murmured softly. 'Good for you, *cara.* Keep the bastard dancing on his toes for as long as you can. He'll break some time and tell you the truth about the Gianni—Carlucci union.' His mouth arrived close to her ear. 'Unless you already know about it, of course, and you keep him dancing as you did me—just for the hell of it.'

She tugged her hand free; he let it go. He was poison, she reminded herself as on a wave of sickness she walked shakily away, weaving through the clutches of people without daring to make eye contact—just in case they'd seen her talking to Angelo.

She made a beeline for the one place she felt safe. He was still talking business with the same two people she'd left him with when she went to find the loo. Coming up beside him, she slipped her hand into his and felt his fingers close instantly. She was trembling. Could he feel she was trembling? He made no sign of it as he talked in velvet dark undertones, which held his audience captivated. She didn't hear a single word. She was too busy trying to filter Angelo's poison from her blood. After a few minutes, Carlo excused them and swapped her hand for her waist to lead her into the adjoining room then onto the dance floor. Music was playing, soft and slow.

His fingertips feathered lightly down her sides and came to settle at the indentation at her waist then he drew her against him. Relieved to be in the arms of the only man she ever wanted to be with, her hands came to rest against his wide shoulders, her unsteady breath warming his throat.

'OK,' he said quietly. 'What did he say to you?'

It was a shock. She hadn't thought he'd seen her talking to Angelo because he'd had his back turned towards the doorway. 'I—you—I didn't know he was going to be here tonight.'

'Neither did I,' he said in a tone that made her blood chill.

'H-he took me by surprise...'

'I can see that,' he drawled. 'You're as white as a sheet and trembling like a leaf.' And he was not happy about it. 'So, what did he say?' he prompted again.

She fixed her eyes on the cleft in his chin and tried another steadying breath. 'Poison,' she said. 'He's made up of pure poison.'

'Is that it?' he said after waiting a minute for her to explain.

'Yes.' She moved that bit closer to his strong, dark frame. 'If I talk about it, Carlo, he will have achieved what he wanted to achieve. And I won't let him.'

'Fair enough.' He didn't push the issue and they left not long after the dance.

But he was silent on the journey back to the apartment and there was a new intensity about his lovemaking that night. He took her swimming close to the edge, only to pull her back from the brink time after time. In the end she had to plead with him before he relented and let her topple into the fierce and furied waterfall of release.

Exhausted afterwards, too weak and boneless to do anything other than breathe, she fell asleep, only to be woken in the dark depths of the night to be pulled through the same intense journey all over again.

CHAPTER TEN

THE next morning she woke up late to find the place beside her in the bed empty and with a hangover that had nothing to do with the few sips of wine she'd had the evening before. Her body ached—inside and out. Her head felt as if it was trying to swim and as she moved sluggishly into the bathroom she felt so dizzy she thought for a few minutes that she was going to be sick.

It took all her energy to get dressed and go to work, feeling the way that she did. The day passed like any other day. She trailed people round the sites of Rome and managed to sound interesting and enthusiastic as she went through her usual routine. But the headache hadn't eased and the sickness lay like a knot in her stomach she couldn't seem to release.

By the time she got back to the apartment she felt so wrecked it was all she could do to strip and shower then crawl between cool cotton sheets.

Carlo found her like that, nothing more than a tumble of dark golden curls lost in a mound of white. He stood looking at her for a long time, his expression made stern by the way he frowned. Then he too stripped off his clothes and went to take a shower. When he came back she heard him moving about and stirred.

'You're back,' she mumbled.

'Mm,' he said. He was pulling on a pair of jeans. 'Too tired to talk to me?' he asked lightly.

'Mm,' she echoed, burrowing deeper into the covers. 'Headache,' she explained. 'Feel a bit sick. Just want to sleep.'

It was the last thing she remembered until she awoke the

next morning feeling a whole lot better. Carlo, the perpetual early riser, was already up. She showered, dressed for work then left the bedroom to go in search of sustenance—starving after her queasy fast of the day before.

But she didn't get as far as the kitchen. Passing his study, she saw Carlo standing behind his desk.

'Morning,' she smiled from the doorway.

'Ciao,' he responded—without a returning smile.

He was dressed for the office in a pale blue shirt, grey trousers and a dark tie. His jacket, she saw, was draped over the back of the chair behind him. Freshly shaven, hair neat, he was holding a stack of papers in his hands, which he was in the process of lining up in a neat column on the desk.

And if she had to epitomise man at his most dynamic then Carlo was it at that moment. 'Sorry about last night,' she murmured. 'I had a headache.'

'So you said.' She watched him select a few more sheets of paper then put them down on the long row.

The atmosphere was strange—cool—and the lack of a smile from him was making her frown. Was he cross with her about last night? He'd barely offered her a glance and his mouth had a flatness about it that suggested he was annoyed about something. He'd slept beside her last night; she had a vague memory of his soothing 'shh' as he'd gathered her close.

'I'm disturbing you,' she said, deciding his preoccupation was with those papers not annoyance with her, and went to turn away.

'No—wait,' he said. 'I need you to sign these for me.'

'Me?' She frowned as she walked forward, looking down at the column of documents and recognised the Carlucci business logo on the top one, but after that she could only see the bottom two inches of each set, bearing the bold scrawl of his own signature. 'What are they?' she asked.

'Mostly bank and store accounts I've opened for you that require your signature,' he answered coolly.

'But I thought you understood I don't want—'

'The point of this particular exercise is not what you want but what I want,' he cut in.

'And you want the Carlucci mistress to have all the right-coloured cards in her purse as befitting her exalted title?' she responded with tart.

'The Carlucci bride would be receiving a lot more.'

She stared at the smooth dark planes of his unsmiling face. Marriage hadn't come up in conversation once since they'd left Castelli Romani. Now here it was being filtered back in beneath the guise of loaded grim sarcasm.

'Neither are you my mistress,' he added curtly, 'so I would prefer you did not refer to yourself in such a way.'

'I will be your mistress if I sign those papers, Carlo,' she stated heavily. 'At the moment I keep myself while I'm living here…'

'Unless, of course, you are forced to come to me like a guilty thief about to rob me because you need extra money to get you through the rest of the month.'

She looked up, blushing at the reminder. Within a few short weeks of living with him here in Rome she'd come to realise how expensive it was to be a wealthy man's lover. Only last week she'd been forced to ask him to lend her some money to get her through the rest of the month until her next salary cheque because she'd blown all she had on haircuts and manicures—and that dress she'd bought on a wicked whim because it promised to raise his temperature gauge.

'It was a one-off loan and I do mean to pay you back,' she insisted defensively. 'And I never meant to prompt you to—'

'This way you don't have to pay me back.' He held out a pen. 'Accept with grace, *cara*,' he advised smoothly.

'You don't look too happy about having to do it.' She folded her arms instead of taking the pen.

'That is because I knew I was in for a fight.'

'H-how much money are we talking about?' she asked warily. He named a monthly allowance that made her gasp. 'But I'll never spend that in a hundred years!'

'You will when you get used to it,' he assured with a touch of cynicism.

'I don't want to get used to it!'

He didn't budge a small inch. 'Sign,' he instructed.

She looked down at the column of documents. There were a dozen of them at least. 'And…' she prompted. 'You said these papers were *mostly* bank and store accounts, what else is there that requires my signature?'

'Some legal stuff to do with you living with me.' He effected a shrug. 'Call it protection against—'

'The mistress with avarice.'

'No.' He leant forward, looking her directly in the eyes for the first time since this strange interview began. 'To protect you if I decide to throw you out in only the clothes you stand up in—which might just happen quite soon if you don't stop being so stubborn,' he threatened darkly.

'I don't need protecting from y-you or anyone.'

'Trust me, *cara*, you should be standing behind bullet-proof glass right now.'

His eyes took on a familiar glitter. She saw seduction as the next form of persuasion being promised to her and felt her senses begin to sting. Would she be able to hold out under one of his sensual onslaughts? No, of course she wouldn't be able to hold out, she informed herself—and snatched the pen from his fingers.

There was little grace or gratitude in the way she penned her name in the appropriate place he indicated with a long finger. The atmosphere hissed and spat with each full stop she stabbed at the end of each signature and each grimly pointed indication of his finger as it moved down the column.

When it was over she threw down the pen and straightened. 'Just think,' she said tartly, 'I get to swan around

Rome playing the pampered bitch that gets doors opened for her and a suitable amount of grovelling because I now possess the appropriate clout.'

'You also get to give up your job,' he included as he gathered in the signed papers with the deft slide of his fingers. 'And instead of coming home to me dead on your feet, you will be here,' he stated, 'rested, beautiful and waiting for me.'

Francesca felt her eyes widen to the fullest in utter incredulity. Was that what this was really all about? She'd spent one measly night neglecting him due to a headache and he responded with—this?

'I'm not giving up my job just because you say so,' she told him. 'No way,' she added as the papers were neatly slotted into a folder then shut away in a drawer. It was one thing letting him dictate just about every other facet of her life but she was not going to let him take away the one small thing she had left that gave her some independence from him!

His hands arrived flat on the cleared desk surface. He ignored the angrily lifted chin and the warning flash from her eyes. 'Not negotiable, *cara.*'

'Then you can keep your money and your—other stuff,' she responded. 'We will continue as we are or not at all!'

With that she turned and walked out of the door then out of the whole apartment with a very satisfying slam of the outer door.

Carlo moved to the window to watch as she appeared in the sunny courtyard. Each tense move she made as she wheeled her scooter between parked cars then climbed onto it told him she was angry enough to drive straight at him if he dared to walk in front of her.

Red dress, red Vespa, red flags in her cheeks...he watched her drive off then uttered a thick, black, bloody curse and turned back to his desk. The folder reappeared with its neatly signed documents. Next he picked up his mobile and began making calls. Ten minutes later he was following her out onto the Corso but where she would have turned into the city he turned out of it with the kind of grim resolve about his driving that left no room for him to worry if she was concentrating properly negotiating the mad traffic that was Rome.

Francesca was too angry to concentrate—and she'd slammed out of the apartment without so much as a cup of coffee to help kick start her day!

He'd done that—Mr Arrogant, who thought he could dictate to her and get away with it.

She glowered at a motorist who cut right in front of her. He—it had to be a man—hit his horn and blew her a kiss. *'Bella—bella!'* he called out then looped his way into the stream of traffic. Men were all the same, she thought as she watched him go. They were all pushy egotists that liked to get their own way.

She parked the Vespa at the rear of the hotel she was to collect her tour group from and because she was a half-hour earlier than she should be, due to storming out without breakfast, she walked to the nearest patisserie and bought a chocolate croissant and a coffee to go. The moment she bit into the croissant she knew she wasn't going to be able to eat it. Even the coffee tasted sour.

His fault, she blamed, dumped the croissant and coffee in the nearest bin and walked back to the hotel. An hour later she was in full professional mode, two hours further on and they'd reached the Trevi Fountain, where she left her group to toss coins and take photographs, while she bought a bottle of chilled water from one of the kiosks and sank down on a nearby bench.

The sun was hot and the crowds were thick; drawing a decent breath was an effort and she was beginning to feel dizzy and sick again.

Maybe she'd caught a bug, she mused as she sat sipping water. It was a big relief to know that this was the last stop on this morning's tour, which meant she had a whole two hours to herself before the afternoon tour began.

She was just considering whether to go back to the apartment to take some painkillers and lie down for a while, when a shadow fell across her. She glanced up—it was instinctive—then instantly wished she hadn't when she saw who it was.

'*Ciao*,' Angelo greeted sombrely. 'I hoped I would find you here today.'

Her heart sank like a stranded whale to her hollow stomach. 'Why did you hope that?' she demanded heavily.

'We need to talk.'

'We've already done that.'

'I know.' He shrugged. It was oddly diffident for him.

Then he seemed to make some monumental decision and sat himself down next to her. Two young girls sharing the same bench were staring at him in open-mouthed awe. He had it all, Francesca observed ruefully, the amazing good looks, the long, lean body perfectly turned out in a lightweight grey suit. The gold streaks in his hair were catching the sunlight and warming his golden skin. He even smelled good, and if he decided to turn his head and offer them an afternoon's wild sex then his two man-struck observers would be his for the taking—it was that obvious.

But he didn't turn his head. With an art taught to any Roman in its cradle he completely ignored that they were sitting there at all. In fact he just sat staring at the Trevi Fountain with his eyes hidden behind the glasses and the relaxed pose he'd adopted doing nothing to hide his tension from her.

Francesca took another sip at the water. Her head was beginning to ache, bright balls of pain propelling themselves at the backs of her eyelids. She really did have a bug of some kind, she told herself wearily and wished she were back in bed.

'Don't marry him,' he said suddenly.

'What?' she gasped, turning to stare at him, not believing she'd heard what he'd just said.

'I know I messed up, and I know I messed you up, but don't make another mistake by marrying him, Francesca.'

'What business is it of yours what I do, Angelo?'

'None.' He grimaced. 'But I could not just turn my back on this, knowing what I do.'

'You don't know anything,' she denied huskily. 'And I'm not marrying anyone, so just leave it alone and go away.'

'Don't lie, *cara*, It is not in your nature. He rang me this morning to tell me,' he added before she could speak. 'You plan to marry next week in the small chapel attached to his *palazzo*.'

She didn't even know there was a chapel attached to the *palazzo*! 'Carlo—told you that?' She gasped in disbelief then felt a funny little flutter gather pace in her stomach as her head threw up a vision of the bad-tempered brute as he'd looked this morning while he bullied her into signing his precious documents.

Had he been planning a surprise wedding for them? Was that what the papers had really been about? Did he intend dragging her off by her hair and forcing her to wear his ring because he knew she would put up a fight otherwise? The flutter altered to a warm glow of humour. The headache began to ease. She even smiled to herself.

'He then went on to warn me off,' Angelo was saying. 'If he sees me in the same room as you again he suggests I will not like the consequences.'

'Then what are you doing sitting here?' she asked him. 'Batistes discovered they can survive without his business, have they?'

'I don't think he was referring to the business side, *cara*; he was meaning my skin.'

So Carlo was jealous of Angelo? Oh, this was getting better and better. Just wait until I get alone with him and I will…

'And I'm sitting here because I've discovered I have a conscience that is overriding my common sense.'

Angelo stole her attention again and dragged off his glasses, revealing those amazing blue eyes that still had the ability to startle when you first looked into them. 'You're so beautiful these days you take my breath away,' he said tensely. 'I regret losing you, *mi amore*. I cannot tell you how much I regret being such a fool. But this isn't about me, it's about you. Don't marry him, Francesca,' he begged urgently. 'He means to hurt you just as badly as I did.'

'No.' She stood up. 'I'm not going to listen to any more of your poison, Angelo.'

He stood up too. 'I might speak poison but I also speak the truth!' he insisted in a harsh undertone. 'He warned me off coming near you because he is scared of what I know!'

'And what do you think you know?' she challenged fiercely. 'That there really is a Gianni fortune stashed away somewhere waiting for me to marry to claim it, and now Carlo is the mercenary rat trying to get his greedy hands on it?'

'Yes,' he hissed. 'I'm sorry, but that's exactly how it is.'

'There is *no* fortune!' She sighed. 'How many times do I have to repeat that to you before you will believe?'

'How many times do I have to tell you there is a fortune for you to inherit before *you* believe?'

'Oh, stop this.' She sighed. 'Even if there was money, unlike you, Carlo doesn't need any more—he has enough of the stuff as it is!'

'Not money,' Angelo conceded. 'But a large block of Carlucci stock has been locked away in your grandfather's estate since he died. Carlo wants it back. He certainly does not want any other man getting control of it.'

'As in—you?'

'As in any other man but himself!' He released a harsh sigh.

She turned away, not wanting to listen any longer but—

'No, don't turn your back on this, Francesca.' Angelo grabbed her arm and spun her back again. 'On my mother's life I am telling you the truth! I don't want your unhappiness on my conscience any longer. I don't want to see you hurt again!'

The headache was getting worse by the second and their two observers were still watching avidly. By their expression they could not understand a word of Italian so had no idea what they were talking about, but that did not stop this from turning into a very public scene!

'But if you cannot bring yourself to believe me then speak to your great-uncle,' Angelo persisted. 'Demand he tell you the truth. Ask him *why* your grandfather's estate has Carlucci stock locked up in it,' he urged huskily. 'Ask him about the Carlucci-Gianni feud that has been going on since your mother jilted his father at the church altar to marry her English gigolo!'

Her head began to spin dizzily. She had no option but to sit down again. Angelo joined her. 'I am not toying with you just for the hell of it,' he continued hurriedly. 'I am in fact risking a great deal by telling you this because Carlo can ruin my family with a single blow.'

She looked up, some hazy part of her professional instinct making her search out her tour group. Eyes barely focusing, she managed to detect them dispersed around the small square, shopping for souvenirs.

'Then why are you doing it?'

'Because I discovered I'm in love with you,' he declared with a self-deprecating grimace. 'Though I had to lose you before I knew it.'

Oddly enough, she actually believed him. She had never heard Angelo sound so grimly sincere. The thing was, did she believe everything else he'd said?

She didn't have an answer to that. She couldn't seem to think of anything clearly right now. Even trying to take the cap off her bottle of water was beyond her. Angelo took it and did it for her while she swallowed thickly on the nausea she could feel building inside. She took a few sips, felt the cool water slide down her throat and into her empty stomach. No warm glow there now, she noticed bleakly.

And she knew at that precise moment that, whether she believed him or not, she was going to have to check his story out.

Pushing herself back to her feet, she swayed a little.

Angelo rose also. 'What are you going to do?' he asked.

'Go and see my great-uncle.' What other choice was there?

'I'll take you,' he offered. 'You cannot want to do that journey on your Vespa and the train station is miles away from your great-uncle's *palazzo*. Let me drive you,' he begged. 'You don't look too good, *cara*,' he added gently when she went to refuse him.

Gentle did it. Gentle made her eyes swim with weak tears and her heart swim with other things—pending agony, she named it. It was preparing itself for what was about to hit. 'OK,' she agreed. 'I h-have to take my tour group back to their hotel first.'

There wasn't a hint of smug triumph about him and if there had been she would have changed her mind about going anywhere with him. 'Tell me which hotel and I'll collect my car and meet you there,' was all he said.

Two hours later Angelo was pulling the car to a stop by her great-uncle's wilderness driveway, after having completed the whole journey in near silence after Angelo's main attempt of, 'Let me explain about—' had been stalled before it got started, by her muted,

'How is it you know so much about the Giannis and me?'

There had been a moment of silence, a flat-line grimace that attacked his mouth. Then, 'Your great-uncle's housekeeper talks to my mother's housekeeper,' he said.

She had nodded, seeing—feeling the import in that reply

like an extra weight trying to suffocate hope. 'I will hear the rest from my uncle,' she told him. And Angelo had respected that.

The gates were shut as always. He was about to climb out of the car to open them but Francesca stopped him.

'Thank you for bringing me, but I want to go on alone from here,' she said.

He turned a frowning look on her. The fact that she was as pale as a ghost didn't pass him by and her mouth was trembling—though she wished that it wouldn't.

'You know I am telling you the truth, don't you?' he murmured.

What could she say? He would have to possess a really twisted sense of humour to go to this amount of trouble on the back of a few lies. But there was one small, tiny glimmer of hope left in her that what he thought he knew was nothing more than rumour getting out of control.

She went to climb out of the car without answering.

'I will wait for you,' he said.

Francesca flashed him a glance. 'You don't have—'

'I said I will wait, *cara,*' he insisted. 'You never know,' he smiled then, 'you might actually be glad to see me by the time you leave here.'

Not in the way she suspected he meant, she thought as he left it at that and climbed out of the car. She could feel his eyes following her as she stepped up to the gates and pushed one of them open. As she closed it behind her again her eyes grazed over the rusty old letterbox that looked as if it hadn't been opened in a hundred years.

The whole place still had that look about it, she thought as she began walking up the vine-strewn driveway beneath the overhanging branches of gnarled old trees. Even the quiet heat of the afternoon had a hushed, undisturbed quality about it, the cracked and peeling frontage of the house wearing the patina of neglect.

Her nerves began to knot as she walked around a huge

rhododendron bush, which kept more than half of the house hidden from the drive. What if her great-uncle refused to see her? What if he refused to answer her questions even if he did condescend to grant her a meeting?

Then she saw the red car parked at the bottom of the crumbling steps that led up to the front door and she knew then—knew that whatever happened next she was going to walk away the loser.

It took her a few moments to come to terms with that, and a few more moments to get anger to override the growing throb of her aching heart. Then she walked around the car and up the steps to use the heavy brass door knocker, grained and pitted with age.

The housekeeper opened the door to her. One glance at Francesca's face and she was lowering her eyes and stepping aside.

'Where are they?' she demanded as she stepped past her.

'The main *sala, signorina.* Where you met with your great-uncle the last time you were here.'

Moving on legs that did not feel very stable, she walked along a threadbare carpet runner and paused outside the *sala* door. Deep breath, she instructed herself. Be ready for what you see. Then she pressed her lips together and opened the door.

They were sitting in cracked leather wing-back chairs by an open fire. The heat in the room was oppressive, though the chill covering her skin kept Francesca feeling like ice. The remains of a lunch of crusty bread and pasta lay spread on a small table and if she was expecting to find two feudal lords confronting each other then she was disappointed. They were sharing a bottle of crisp dry Frascati wine and could not appear more at ease with each other as they sat there talking as if they'd been close friends for a lifetime.

Carlo was the first one to see her standing there. He shot to his feet, looking everything she wished that he wasn't, which was tall and dark and so unbearably handsome her heart tilted over and gave a squeeze of quiet agony.

'Francesca,' he breathed in surprise.

Don't speak to me, she wanted to shout but didn't dare say anything to him while she was feeling so raw. So she turned to look to her great-uncle Bruno, whose silver head took its time turning and the eyes—so like her own—remained calm as they looked back at her.

Why couldn't you like me? she thought helplessly and had to curl her fingers into her palms before she could utter a word. 'I believe you have something to tell me,' she prompted.

'I do?' Silver eyebrows rose in a typical Latin gesture. 'As far as I am aware, *signorina*, I have nothing of importance to say to you.'

'Francesca—'

No, *don't*! She flashed Carlo a wild, bright, silencing look—then looked back at her great-uncle. 'Just tell me,' she demanded. 'Am I or am I not the sole beneficiary to my grandfather's fortune?'

'Not as you stand here now, *signorina*,' he replied ambiguously.

'When I marry, then,' she said tensely.

'Are you married?'

'No, I am not married and not planning to be,' she flashed out. 'And why can't you just answer me without turning it into a—?'

Carlo shifted on a sigh. '*Cara*, don't turn this into a drama. There is an explanation as to why—'

'You're here?' She turned on him tensely. 'As to why you—and all of Rome—know more about me than I know about myself? Tell me, Carlo, how long did it take your father to recover from my mother's desertion before he went to Paris and married his child bride?'

'Who has been talking to you?' He frowned suddenly.

Francesca tugged in an unsteady breath of air. 'What does

it matter who's been talking when I only need to ask any stranger on the Corso to find out that my mother jilted your father to marry my father and that Bruno Gianni is a nasty, sneaky, miserable old man!'

'Hah,' Bruno Gianni laughed. 'She has spirit, that one, just like a Gianni. You have trouble on your hands, Carlo, if you mean to tame the child.'

'I am not a child,' she flung at him next. 'And Signor Carlucci is dead in my eyes. Is that Gianni enough for you?'

'*Sì,*' the old man nodded seriously. 'Your grandfather would be proud of you.'

'Why won't you tell me what I need to know?' she quavered suddenly and knew she was about to lose control.

'Because his hands are tied by your grandfather's will,' Carlo provided. 'He is not allowed to discuss it with you until you comply with its terms.'

'How can I comply when I don't know what those terms are?' she cried.

'Precisely,' Carlo said. 'The Giannis are not known for making life easy for anyone, *cara.*'

'Have we moved on to discuss Carlucci stock now?'

Carlo cursed. 'Who *has* been talking to you?'

'Batiste?' her great-uncle suggested helpfully.

'He would not dare,' Carlo said narrowly. 'I warned him off this…'

Francesca's face gave her away. And that was the point when Carlo's mood changed. 'How did you get here, *cara*?' he demanded thinly. 'You don't look as if you rode ninety kilometres on a Vespa.'

She looked as pristine and neat as she had when she stormed out on him this morning—except for her face, Carlo saw. Her skin was pale and her eyes looked bruised. Pining for her lost love? Or was the look down to guilt because the lost love had returned? he wondered cynically, and felt his teeth grind together behind his taut lips.

'You've been with him,' he rasped in accusation. 'You came here with him!'

'Maybe he loves me after all,' she said defiantly. 'Maybe we stopped on the way here to indulge in some—'

He moved like streaked lightning. She didn't even see him coming until his hands landed on her shoulders. 'Carlo—*amico*,' Bruno murmured in protest but he barely registered the words.

'Take that back or I will kill you both,' he growled furiously.

She was trembling all over but her chin went up, her eyes bright with both anger and tears. 'Vendettas all round, *caro*?' she taunted.

'There are no vendettas!' he rasped. 'But if you don't withdraw what you just said to me I will turn this into one!'

'Why don't you confess your sins to me then I will confess mine?'

'I don't have any sins to confess to!'

'You've been lying to me. You've been making love to me for weeks and weeks as if I meant something special to you but all you really wanted was—this!'

Her voice had risen to a shrill pitch by the time she'd finished. 'You are getting me mixed up with Batiste,' he gritted.

'Are you saying there is no Carlucci stock locked up in my grandfather's estate?'

He breathed and let go of her before he did something stupid. Then had to watch her quiver and sway then put a pale hand up to cover her eyes. Had he hurt her? Had his fingers bitten too hard? '*Cara*...' he murmured roughly.

'No, don't come near me.' She held up her free hand to ward against him. 'I need to...' pull myself together and finish this, Francesca thought desperately. Because she'd just remembered something else and it was making her feel sick to her stomach.

She looked up at him through the bruised eyes of pain. 'What did you really get me to sign this morning?'

He turned away. She saw attention caught by her great-uncle Bruno, who had sat through it all, listening with interest. There was an exchange of glances. She couldn't see what Carlo's look was saying but she read her great-uncle's get-out-of-this-one expression.

'Tell me,' she whispered.

'You signed your life away,' he informed her sardonically. 'You can marry who the hell you want to but your fortune will be controlled by me.'

The air in the room suddenly felt oppressive, the heat from the fire and the intensity of Carlo's silence weighing on her aching head. The walls tried to close in. Grimly she pushed them back again. I've got to get out of here before I completely humiliate myself by fainting at his feet, she thought hazily.

'OK.' She nodded then had to swallow thickly when the foolish head movement sent her dizzy. 'Then I won't marry.'

'Oh, don't restrict yourself so, *signorina*,' her great-uncle Bruno lazily put in. 'If you don't want your grandfather's fortune then you only need to stay away from Italian men from good families.'

'Stay out of this, Bruno!' Carlo raked at the old man. 'You are not supposed to speak about it!'

'Seems futile to remain silent if Francesca has no wish to inherit,' the old man pointed out.

'Which pleases you because you get to go on living here for free.'

'True,' Bruno agreed. 'Until I die, when the money goes to charity.'

Charity, Francesca repeated to herself and almost found a bleak little smile. This whole set-up was one huge, self-seeking charity.

'Well, good luck to you, *signor*,' she murmured politely.

'I hope you enjoy the lonely comfort of the rest of your life.'

With that she turned and walked back into the hallway. She heard Carlo angrily hiss her name but didn't stop her from walking away. She'd had it with Rome. She was going to go home—to England—and never set foot on Italian soil again.

CHAPTER ELEVEN

CARLO didn't come after her. She didn't know if that made her hurt all the more or if she was just aching with relief. Whichever, there were tears in her eyes as she stepped outside into the dappled sunlight and she felt as though she was floating as she walked down the drive.

Angelo was leaning against his car when she stepped through the gate again. He took one look at her face and was leaping into action, striding round the car to open the passenger door for her then grimly watching her as she slipped silently into the seat.

'Where to now?' he asked as he got in beside her.

He wasn't even going to ask if everything he'd said had been confirmed in there, she realised. But then he didn't need to. For once Angelo felt secure in his truth.

'Back to Rome,' she said. 'I—need to pack my things.'

'Then what?'

She shrugged, not wanting to think that far ahead.

'Why don't we go to the villa?' he suggested huskily. 'It's only a couple of miles from here and you look as if you need—'

'Rome, please, Angelo,' she put in firmly. 'Or you can drop me off at the train station if you don't want to drive back there tonight.'

He didn't even bother to answer that. Grimly firing the car engine, he fed it into gear and turned them around to go back the way they had come. Within minutes the smooth motion of the car sent her sleepy, the headache, stress and now a throbbing heartache dragging her down into a dark place that kept her huddled and motionless in the seat beside Angelo while he drove.

She didn't stir again until her senses picked up the scents and sounds of the city. Sliding upright in her seat, she looked out on the half-light of the summer evening to discover they were moving down the river embankment.

Pulling in through the archway to Carlo's apartment building, Angelo stopped and killed the engine then glanced outside.

'His car isn't here.'

'No.' Even Carlo couldn't be in two places at the same time, she thought bleakly.

'Thanks for giving up half your day for me.' She reached for the door lock.

'Look,' he turned in his seat. 'I can't just drop you here and drive away without knowing you're OK, *cara*. Go and pack a bag. I'll wait here for you. Then you can come and stay with me while you decide what—'

'Sorry, Angelo,' she cut in. 'But whatever you're hoping to gain from today, it isn't going to be me.'

'I never meant—'

'I know exactly what you meant, *caro*,' she said gently, then climbed out of the car. His side-window came down as she walked past it. An arm appeared with a set of long golden fingers that gently caught her hand. Her beautiful golden man, she thought sadly as she paused to look down at him—and felt nothing.

Nothing.

'You're in love with him, aren't you?'

'Surprise, surprise,' she mocked then felt the tears fill her eyes.

'I'm sorry.'

'What for—opening my eyes for me…again?'

His sigh was accompanied by a wince. 'I messed up big time.'

So did I. 'Thanks for driving me.' Slipping her hand free, she walked on, and didn't look back again even though she knew he watched her all the way until she'd disappeared inside the building.

The first thing she did on entering the apartment was go straight to the bathroom to take a couple of painkillers.

The second thing she did was strip off her clothes and stand beneath the shower for ages, just emptying her mind of everything.

The third thing she did was wrap herself in a long white terry bathrobe, then went to find her small suitcase, threw it down on the bed, sat down beside it—and burst into tears.

Carlo arrived in the open bedroom door after the crying fit was over and she was packing her case. His jacket had gone, as had his tie, and he was looking just a bit worn round the edges, she noticed in the one very brief glance she allowed herself to offer him before turning away. His hair was ruffled and he looked tired and grim but not particularly bothered to find her packing to leave him.

That hurt, but then everything was hurting—throbbing head, aching heart, painful—

'Where are you going to go?' he questioned levelly.

'A hotel for now,' she replied coolly. 'Then back to England, where I intend to get on with my life.'

'Starting it by finding a strictly English man to marry just to get back at me?'

'You said it.' She shrugged and walked away into her dressing room, where she spent a few minutes carefully selecting only the clothes she had bought herself.

When she came back into the bedroom he was still standing there with a shoulder resting casually against the door jamb, arms folded, feet crossed in classical Carlo Carlucci look-how-relaxed-I-am-about-this pose.

'I won't stop you from leaving, you know,' he told her.

'I don't want you to stop me.' She sent him a false smile and dropped an armload of clothes onto the bed.

'But I will not allow it to finish like this.'

'Because you want your Carlucci stock back.' She packed two skirts and a jacket without even knowing it.

'The stock is incidental.'

'Like the control of it you got me to sign away?' Several other items of clothing went the same way.

'You needed protecting.'

'From whom, for goodness' sake?' she turned to flash at him, then spun away again because it still hurt too much to look at him and the tears were trying to come back but— not this time, she told them fiercely. I will not cry in front of him ever again! 'The only person I need protecting from around here is you,' she declared huskily. 'I trusted you, Carlo. In spite of everything I went through with Angelo, I trusted you to be honest with me.'

'I was honest,' he snapped. 'As far as I could be,' he added. 'Would you like to know how it was that I became involved with you in the first place?'

Shoes, she'd forgotten shoes, she realised, and walked back into the dressing room, ignoring his offer of an explanation as if hadn't spoken at all. Then she just stood there with her hands clenched and her eyes tightly closed, trembling like a pathetic, weak-minded idiot because she wanted to hear his explanation more than anything if it was going to justify what he'd done.

But how could he justify it? her cynical side put in. He was just another taker like Angelo, probably willing to say anything if it got him what he wanted from her.

Which was a block of measly stock with a bit of revenge thrown in because her mother had jilted his father twenty-four years ago. She felt sick again.

No, she didn't, she then told her dipping stomach and grimly forced open her eyes and selected two pairs of shoes at random.

When she went back to the bedroom her case had gone. She stopped dead in her tracks. The bedroom door had been open before but it was now firmly shut and the brass key had disappeared from the lock. Her eyes flickered to where Carlo was now standing by the bed, casually feeding his wrist-watch into the bedside-cabinet drawer.

Her turned a glance on her, her skin began to prickle, her pulse dropping to a low, slow throb. Provocation was written into every single challenging pore of him. She glanced around the room. The suitcase was nowhere. She looked back at him.

'You said you weren't going to stop me from leaving,' she murmured warily.

'I changed my mind.' He began to unbutton his shirt.

'Any reason worth hearing?' She tried for sarcasm but didn't quite pull it off.

'Sex is a good enough reason for me, *cara*,' he drawled lazily. 'But I think you might need a bit of convincing before you will agree.'

She stared at him, hovering like an idiot because she wasn't quite sure what to do next. The shirt was slowly revealing a long male torso, rich in the sensually masculine sweep of crisp dark hair.

'Please don't do that,' she tremored.

The shirt landed like a challenge on the floor by his feet.

'I'm going to take a shower before we finish this,' he announced and turned towards the bathroom, tanned muscles glossed with the sweat of a long day and flexing with a tension he was trying to pretend he didn't have.

'Carlo, please don't—'

He turned on her like a panther on the attack. Even the snap of his white teeth scared the life out of her as he covered the space between them, snatched the shoes from her hands, dropped them then picked her up by the waist.

She landed on the bed without really knowing how she'd got there. 'What do you think—?'

He arrived then, one hard, angry male accompanied by one hard, angry kiss. She groaned beneath the pressure of it, then whimpered because she knew she was going to respond.

He saved her that indignity by lifting his dark head to glare at her. 'Now, listen to me, you broken-hearted idiot,' he ground out. 'I am not your enemy and I never have been.'

'Y-you plotted against me.'

'I plotted *for* you!' he amended fiercely. 'Bruno called me in as soon as you wrote to tell him you were going to marry Batiste.'

'He's as bad as you are!'

'Who? Bruno or Batiste?'

'Both!' she cried and tried to wriggle herself free.

His eyes darkened. 'You don't want to do that, *amore*, if you don't want this to move on to its inevitable conclusion just yet.'

Sheer fury at his confidence made her hit out with her fists. Both were caught and pinned above her head with a hand while the other hand firmly cupped her chin.

'The Batistes are in serious financial trouble,' he told her. 'That huge white marble museum of a villa they own has been a drain on their resources since they inherited it. The last time Alessandro came to me for a loan I advised him to give the house away to the country and let them open it to the public—which would mean the Batiste name would keep its damn kudos and they would not be such slaves to the place. No,' he rasped when she tried to speak, 'you don't say anything—you just listen.'

Then he kissed her again just to punctuate which of them was in control here. 'I hate you,' she managed.

'Don't you just,' he mocked, adding a smile because her mouth was still quivering with pleasure from the kiss.

'Angelina Batiste loves that house more than she loves her husband and son,' he went on. 'She would sell them before she would sell it, which is basically what she did. When your name came up in conversation between her and Angelo, she leapt at the opportunity to do a bit of match-

making—with some subtle blackmail thrown in to keep
Angelo in line. He's like Villa Batiste, Francesca. He con-
sumes money faster than he can earn it. He drives a top-of-
the-range car and lives in a top-of-the-range apartment—all
bought on credit, of course. He's handsome but vain, which
makes him very high maintenance. The designer stores rub
their hands together when they see him coming.'

'I suppose you're not high maintenance?'

'I can afford to be. I do not spend above my means!'

'But your stock still languishes in my grandfather's bank
vault! We all crave what we can't have.'

'And what do you crave, *mi amore*—the man you have
spent half the day with or the man who pins you to this
bed?'

'What do you care?' She glared at him. 'You couldn't
even make the effort to stop me driving away with him!'

'Ah,' he said and rolled away from her.

She should have got up while she had the chance—but
she didn't.

'He drives like a maniac. You are lucky he got you here
in one piece.'

She turned her head to stare at him. 'You mean you followed us?'

He turned to look at her. 'Two cars behind you all the
way,' he said.

She frowned as she studied the half-mocking gleam in his
rich, dark eyes. 'Then why didn't you follow us into the
courtyard?'

'Because,' he answered softly, 'I wanted to see what you
were going to do next.'

'Do next in what way?'

'As in whether you packed a bag then left with him or
you gave him short shrift and sent him on his way,' he
explained.

'I don't understand.'

'No, I can see that you don't.' Closing the gap between

their mouths, he stole a quick kiss from her then sat up, leaving her lying there with her lips tingling and what was beginning to feel like a permanent puzzled frown.

He moved then, stretching and flexing those wonderful back muscles like a body builder putting on a show. Her mouth ran dry, her tongue snaked out to coil a lick around her lips.

'Explain,' she said.

'Later,' he said and got to his feet. 'I need that shower—'

'No!' Sitting up, she scrambled to her feet too. 'Explain now!' she insisted.

He swung round to look at her, his dark eyes brooding on her tense, challenging pose. Sudden tension in his face made the bones in his cheeks stand out, not with anger but with—

'You are still in love with him,' he grated.

Her eyes widened. 'I am not!' she denied.

'Don't lie to me,' he said harshly. ' I saw what it did to you when you met him the other night.'

'Shocked—disgusted me?' she suggested.

He flashed her a bitter look. 'Enough for you to whisper his name while you were sleeping in my arms?'

'I couldn't have,' she gasped.

'Well, you did,' he declared. 'You let me make love to you but you fell asleep afterwards with his name on your lips—and if you thought, *cara*, that I was going to stand by and let you swap from me back to him without doing something to protect you from the bastard, then you don't know me at all!'

'You mean you…?' she stopped, tried to think then swallowed before beginning again. 'You mean you tricked me into signing those papers because you thought I was going to go back to him?'

'I told him this morning he would not be touching a penny belonging to you. Clearly, he did not believe me.'

'Y-you also told him you and I were getting married.'

'Why not?' he challenged. 'Would you expect me to hand you over without a fight?'

'I don't know.' She blinked. 'I don't think I know anything of any certainty right now. You've been twisting me in knots since the first time I met you.'

'Knots?' he repeated. 'You want to know about being tied in knots, Francesca, then try being me for a moment or two,' he ground out cynically. 'Because the first time we met I only needed to take one look at you to fall in love so fast I didn't know what had hit me, but you were so starry-eyed over that bastard that you didn't even notice! And that is what I call being *twisted* in knots, which is a hell of a lot worse than just being tied!'

With that he turned and slammed into the bathroom, leaving her standing there frozen by what he'd said. She stood unmoving while she listened to the shower running, remained exactly where she was through every sound that seeped through the bathroom door until he reappeared again, hair wet, clean-shaven, droplets of water clinging to his skin now and a towel clinging to his lean hips.

'I noticed you,' she pushed out, bringing him to a stop. 'I noticed and noticed you!' she extended on a helpless choke. 'I dreamed about you and felt so guilty about doing it that I used to push my head beneath the pillow to hide in shame!'

'You don't have to say this.' He frowned impatiently. 'I don't need pacifying.'

'But it's the truth!' she swore. 'I w-wanted you in a way I never wanted Angelo. I used to hate you being in the same room because I sometimes couldn't cope! You were up there,' she flung a hand out. 'Way beyond me in every way I could think of. And I was committed to another man I was supposed to be in love with, so how could I go home at night and ache for you? S-so I pretended to myself that I didn't like you, that what I was feeling was hostility, that was all. Then we met at those traffic lights and I couldn't pretend anything any more!'

'Don't,' he warned gruffly, 'turn the tears on.'

'But I don't know what else to do!' she cried. 'You say I twisted you in knots but how do you think it felt for me to find out I was falling in love with you? And you *did* play me like a puppet!' she accused him. 'You're still doing it now by standing there waiting for me to grovel when I don't want to grovel! Because I still think you—'

'That's it,' he said and reached out with a hand to grab a chunk of white towelling at her throat then used it to yank her close. 'No need to grovel, Francesca; just shut up and kiss me.'

So she did. She kissed him until they had no clothes on and she kissed him as they tumbled on the bed. She kissed him as she rode him with a fierce, desperate, hungry passion that held him utterly her captive then he reversed their positions and gave back to her what she had given him.

'We marry next week,' he informed her lazily much later.

'In the chapel I don't know about on your *palazzo*?'

He was silent for a moment, then, 'I am going to have to make Batiste keep his nose out of my business,' he said.

'Would my mother have married your father there too?'

He wasn't slow, he knew what she was prompting here. 'OK,' he rolled to lie beside her, 'this is it, the final explanation, so listen carefully because I have better things I want to do with you than talk about other people,' he warned. 'Our parents came together in a business arrangement that revolved around the Carlucci company needing an urgent injection of cash and your grandfather wanting a husband for his daughter. Your mother was never happy with the arrangement so when she met and fell in love with your father she refused to marry anyone else but Vincent Bernard. It caused one hell of a scandal at the time, especially when she fell pregnant. By then our company stock was already in your grandfather's possession. Being a contrary devil, he blamed my father for not getting in there first and making your mother pregnant. Yes,' he nodded when Francesca gasped, 'you can be shocked. My father was shocked too. He told your grandfather a few home truths about his morals, to which your grandfather responded by refusing to sell us back our stock. We have remained on the Gianni black list ever since then—until you came along and frightened Bruno by telling him you were going to marry Angelo Batiste. Suddenly a Carlucci was useful to a Gianni and Bruno thought he had the perfect bargaining tool with our block of stock.'

'So you came hunting me because of a business arrangement with Bruno.'

'No, you suspicious little witch,' he chided. 'I came hunting because I had *already* seen you and already wanted what I saw! You can keep the Carlucci stock locked up forever if it pleases you, *cara*; I don't care.' He rolled again to arrive back on top of her to add lazily, 'So long as you keep me locked up with it.'

'Like a slave?'

'Mm,' he murmured with seductive promise.

'OK,' she agreed. 'Then consider yourself locked up.'

'Good,' he said. 'Great,' he added. 'Then that brings an end to it all.'

'Just like that?'

'*Sì*, just like that.' He nodded. 'I love you. You love me. Your great-uncle Bruno is very happy because I promised not to throw him out of your house. Angelo will be happy because I will promise not to ruin his family business so long as he forgets he knows your name. Now, do you want me to run you a bath so you can relax and recuperate before I ravish you again, or do I get to do more ravishing first?'

Francesca pushed her head back into the pillows so she could look into his handsome, sardonic face and wondered how she was going to live the rest of her life with so much arrogance?

Easy, she told herself. 'Oh, why wait?' she said to him. 'Let's do the ravishing. You know you'll only do it anyway the moment I hit the bath.'

'I knew you were on my wavelength from the moment I set eyes on you.' He smiled in satisfaction, and the ravishing began.

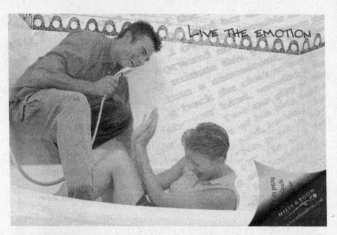

LIVE THE EMOTION

Modern Romance™
...international affairs
– seduction and
passion guaranteed

Medical Romance™
...pulse-raising
romance – heart-
racing medical drama

Tender Romance™
...sparkling, emotional,
feel-good romance

Sensual Romance™
...teasing, tempting,
provocatively playful

Historical Romance™
...rich, vivid and
passionate

Blaze Romance™
...scorching hot
sexy reads

27 new titles every month.

Live the emotion

MILLS & BOON®

MB4

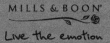

GRAHAM/RTL/1

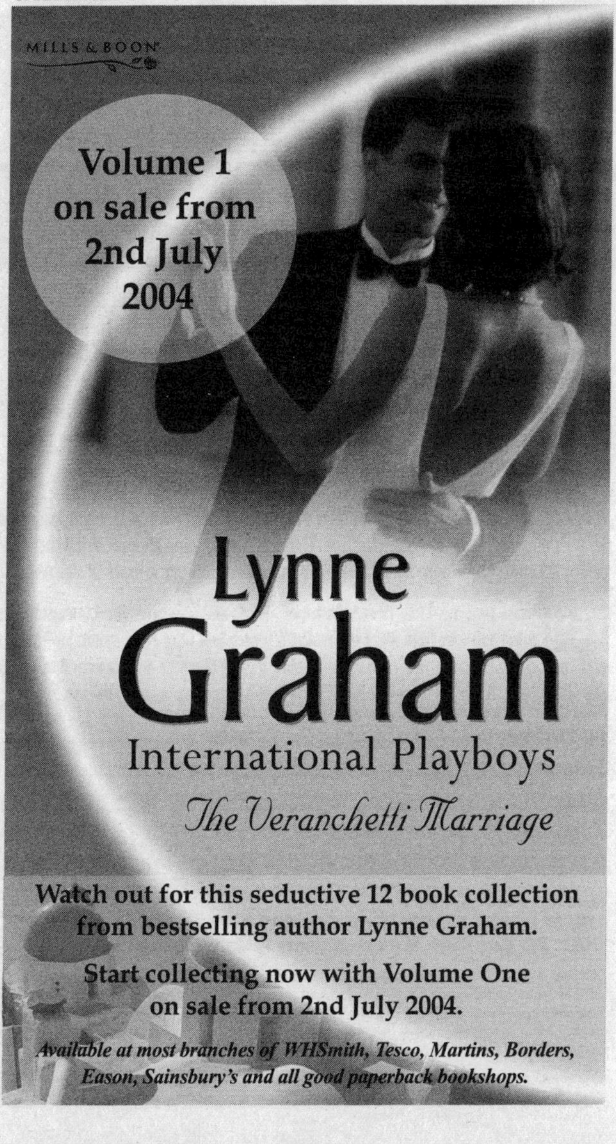
MILLS & BOON
Volume 1 on sale from 2nd July 2004
Lynne Graham
International Playboys
The Veranchetti Marriage
Watch out for this seductive 12 book collection from bestselling author Lynne Graham.
Start collecting now with Volume One on sale from 2nd July 2004.
Available at most branches of WHSmith, Tesco, Martins, Borders, Eason, Sainsbury's and all good paperback bookshops.

FREE
4 BOOKS
AND A SURPRISE GIFT!

We would like to take this opportunity to thank you for reading this Mills & Boon® book by offering you the chance to take FOUR more specially selected titles from the Modern Romance™ series absolutely FREE! We're also making this offer to introduce you to the benefits of the Reader Service™—

- ★ FREE home delivery
- ★ FREE monthly Newsletter
- ★ FREE gifts and competitions
- ★ Exclusive Reader Service discount
- ★ Books available before they're in the shops

Accepting these FREE books and gift places you under no obligation to buy; you may cancel at any time, even after receiving your free shipment. Simply complete your details below and return the entire page to the address below. *You don't even need a stamp!*

YES! Please send me 4 free Modern Romance™ books and a surprise gift. I understand that unless you hear from me, I will receive 6 superb new titles every month for just £2.69 each, postage and packing free. I am under no obligation to purchase any books and may cancel my subscription at any time. The free books and gift will be mine to keep in any case.

P4ZEF

Ms/Mrs/Miss/Mr ....Initials ....
BLOCK CAPITALS PLEASE

Surname ....

Address ....

....

....Postcode ....

Send this whole page to:
UK: FREEPOST CN81, Croydon, CR9 3WZ
EIRE: PO Box 4546, Kilcock, County Kildare (stamp required)